THE DOCTOR
CORNER AND OTHER
GHOST STORIES

SPINE-TINGLING TALES OF
THE SUPERNATURAL

TINA VANTYLER

Published by Zanderam London Press
First printing: 2022
Paperback ISBN: 978-1-7399072-7-3
© Tina Vantyler, 2022
Website: tinavantylerbooks.com

To my very patient family, plus all you wonderful people who read my books.

CONTENTS

One

The Doctor At Cutting Corner

1995

THE SINS OF THE fathers...

Although Alice's boyfriend, Hugo, believed his dad to be blameless in this instance, the shop woman had other ideas.

'You're his son, aren't you,' she stated, not exactly slamming his change on the counter, but setting it down with more force than was necessary. 'From Nathwaite Corner.' A 20p piece rolled off onto the floor, landing with a chink by Alice's foot.

'If you mean Dr Gastrell, then yes, I am,' Hugo replied, looking boldly into her face as he packed groceries into the carrier bag. Alice stooped to retrieve the coin.

Gazing sideways at Hugo, Alice thought of his

1

father, whom she'd met a couple of times. The pair shared the same sharp, intelligent eyes, dimpled chin and ebony hair, parted at the side and as sleek as a cat's fur. Same air of entitlement and superiority. The sins of the fathers indeed. Yet Hugo had a sweetness his father lacked.

Hugo and Alice had met on a London magazine and, after they'd lost their jobs along with a handful of other writers in their department, the boozy evenings commiserating while zipping through their redundancy payments had led to the two of them becoming a couple. And when Hugo asked her to his father's new house to do some decorating – 'Dad will pay us,' he promised – she saw it as a chance to get to know her former colleague properly, as well as earning some much-needed cash.

'Saw his photo in the paper,' continued the woman, narrowing eyes under wispy grey brows at Hugo. 'You look just like him. That poor lady.'

To one side, a girl with her back to them arranging packets of biscuits on a table stopped to listen, flicking a long strand of buttery hair over her shoulder.

Placing a box of eggs on top of the other food, Hugo

said steadily, 'The girl was a known troublemaker, an hysteric, and my father was cleared of all charges.' Not that it has anything to do with *you*, Alice wanted to add, but given that they'd just arrived in the village, they weren't out to make enemies.

Biscuit Girl's shoulders began to shake, as though with amusement.

'Oh, aye, and that's why he was struck off,' said the woman. 'And now he's moving down this way. London folk with their second houses! Then the likes of my girl here have to live elsewhere 'cos the prices have gone through the roof!'

The biscuit arranging picked up again and her daughter's shoulders slumped.

Alice could tell by the muscle twitching in Hugo's jaw that he was furious but doing his best to remain calm. 'Dad hasn't been struck off. He's taking time out to recuperate after the stress of the, um, case and he's bought this place for the family to unwind in.' And unless your girl has quarter of a million quid, she wouldn't have bought that house, thought Alice. 'The property had been on the market over three years,' continued Hugo. 'From the photos I've seen, at least Dad has begun to change that crumbling eyesore into something that looks good. Providing employment for local tradespeople, too.'

The woman mellowed a little. 'Aye, true enough. My Walter was grateful for the work. And no one around here had the money to buy it after Millicent died.'

Alice spoke for the first time. 'Millicent?'

As did Biscuit Girl, turning her small features towards them. 'Millicent Almaric was born in that house and her family owned it for two generations. She couldn't afford the upkeep after her dad died, and it began to fall apart. It's not haunted though – don't worry!' She giggled at her joke.

Her mother pulled a face. 'D' you know, another doctor lived there before the Almarics – I forget his name. He built the house, in the 1800s.'

'Yes,' said Hugo, 'we know about that. Dr Montmorency Clement, who developed certain surgical techniques. My dad admired him greatly and was thrilled to buy his former home.'

Shop Woman suppressed some emotion – distain? 'Yes, well,' she said, straight-faced.

Alice and Hugo made their way to the door, unsure of how to part from someone who'd been so overfamiliar and rude, but whose services Hugo's family would have to rely on as the woman ran the village's only grocery shop. Biscuit Girl muttered something as they passed her.

'Bye then,' Hugo called to the pair as they stepped onto the street.

'What did that girl say?' he asked Alice outside. 'Did you hear?'

Alice scowled. 'I think it was, "That Dr Clement was another wrong 'un."'

It had been drizzling when the pair had entered the shop. That had turned into driving rain so heavy that the 20-minute walk to the house left them with soggy feet inside their city shoes, their hooded coats dripping.

'Two cemeteries so far and only one shop?' said Alice as they turned down the lane which, according to the waterlogged map they'd studied under the shelter of a tree, led to the cottage. 'What does that say about the place?'

'It says,' replied Hugo, turning to her with water

dripping appealingly off the end of his pointed nose, which he wiped away with his fingers, 'that Dad is getting sick of the rat race in London, chasing patients and ever more responsible, stressful posts, and wants a quiet life in a rural location. He may even move down here permanently and get a job at the local cottage hospital.'

I didn't ask about your dad, thought Alice. I asked about the village. But everything seemed to be about Hugo and his family to him. Still, she was developing feelings for the guy, so gave him a peck on his damp cheek. He chuckled and took her hand, pulling her forward. 'Come on, before we fall into a ditch and drown!'

They rounded a hedge on a sharp bend and there, suddenly, was Nathwaite Corner. Taller than it was wide, it loomed up ahead of them, the mottled, pitted grey of a gravestone. Why would you build a house the colour of depression? Alice thought. 'It looks tatty on the outside,' said Hugo, marching down the short path to the front door, 'but quite a bit's been done inside and the gas and electrics have been sorted.'

'Bloody good job,' said Alice. 'Given that it's

February, we couldn't stay here with no lights or heating.' She stood back while Hugo dug in his rucksack for the key, hoping she hadn't made a terrible mistake.

Rather than the fairy-tale cottage with a thatched roof, trellis porch twined with roses and a charming, crooked chimney, Nathwaite Corner looked like the sort of house you drew as a child – plain, with a slate roof and four windows at boring regular intervals. A white door stood in the centre, its paint flaking like psoriasis scales. Here and there patches of peeling plaster showed someone had made a half-hearted attempt to smarten up the exterior.

'Here we go.' Moments later, they stood in a long hall. Taking in oatmeal walls with their heavily embossed paper and floorboards the colour of treacle scattered with threadbare, patterned rugs in faded reds from another age, Alice felt her heart sink even further.

'This place is Dad's boyhood dream,' said Hugo in answer to her downcast expression. 'Thanks to the Almarics taking it straight after the doctor, it retains most of its original features, including some of the wallpaper and carpets. Dad brought his parents' antique furniture out of storage to add to the charm and the Almarics left a few pieces behind.'

'What does your mum think?' asked Alice.

'It will grow on her.'

In other words, Mrs Gastrell had had very little say in it because her husband earned the money – and then some. Since the hearing of Dr Gastrell's case and his recent exoneration, Hugo's mother had fled to her parents' place with his kid brother and sister, while Dr Gastrell had booked a fortnight in Madeira to soothe his nerves.

Down the hall was the parlour, with its rosebud wallpaper and bulky curtains. Alice poked her head around the door, then, in response to Hugo's call, headed to a large kitchen, squelching in after him.

The two radiators looked out of place in the stone-flagged kitchen with its ceiling-height antique Welsh dresser, but Alice was soon grateful that Hugo had successfully tackled the knobs tucked into the boiler cupboard to get the heating belting out from them. Steam rose from their wet coats and socks draped over the radiators, sending a damp dog smell drifting through the room as they each towelled their hair.

Alice opened the cupboards and fridge to put away the bags of food, noting with satisfaction that, even if Hugo's dad wanted to return to a time of lost innocence, at least he'd included a microwave in his rural idyll.

It had been a long train journey from London to the Midlands, followed by a taxi ride to the shop at Emebury Village. After stowing her essentials in the dressing table drawers in the rather gloomy bedroom Hugo showed her to, Alice was too tired to think about anything once they'd downed the macaroni cheese ready meals, eaten with a fork from the plastic containers. They vowed to explore the house properly in the morning.

Sex was quick and lazy in the surprisingly comfortable big bed. Afterwards, Hugo was asleep almost before he'd rolled off her, turning to snuggle into the pillow. Sleepily, Alice hauled the quilt up to her nose and lay listening to the creaks of the old house settling around them. Outside, the rain was soft against the window, as though someone was brushing the panes with fingertips to lull her to sleep. This will be good for us, she thought as she drifted off. See how compatible we really are. See if I really can be part of this family.

She woke to find Hugo at the side of the bed, beaming and holding out a cup of tea. 'Here you go, Milady,' he said, placing it carefully on the side table. 'I've got the paint pots and dust sheets from the shed and made pancakes and bacon to fortify us for the morning's work. Chop chop, before it gets cold!'

It was Saturday and the morning smelt fresh and green after the night of rain, even in the kitchen with the door shut. As they ate, Alice began to feel mean that she was basically road-testing Hugo for long-term relationship potential, even marriage, when he'd already made it plain he considered her to be The One, even after just two months together. She wasn't going to jump in with both feet given that's what her mother had done with what, three men since Alice's dad had died? Alice wanted her marriage to last.

Hugo put their bowls in the sink and handed her a paint-splattered overall to put over her clothes. As she was climbing into it and twisting her russet curls into a knot, the phone in the hall rang and Hugo left to answer it. She heard him talking and marvelled at how quiet the house was, as though it absorbed sounds. She'd have to check how far their nearest neighbour was, in case of emergencies. *Such as what?* She wasn't sure, but it was wise to be prepared.

'That was Dad, checking we have everything we need,' said Hugo, reappearing with stepladders. 'Lucky him, off to the sun. He's at the airport.'

He leaned the ladders on the wall outside the kitchen. 'Let's look around the house. It's my first time too and so far we've only seen the front parlour, kitchen, bathroom and one bedroom!'

A quick glance in the large parlour revealed heavy velvet drapes at the window, a plump sofa and a pair of matching chairs plus a round dining table covered in a berry-coloured cloth with two candlesticks in the centre and four chairs tucked under it. A TV and video machine sat on a tall mahogany chest of drawers. Next, they approached the back room, the door to which was closed. Hugo grasped the knob and had to rattle it and push hard to get the door to swing wide. Unlike the opulently furnished room they'd just left, this even larger space had plain walls in a dirty cream, no rugs on the varnished floor and was devoid of furniture. The tobacco-coloured cotton curtains were drawn and the room was dark with a chilly air.

Alice shivered as Hugo strode across the floorboards and dragged the curtains back, letting in cold morning light, which streaked the floor. 'Dad doesn't know what this room was used for. The estate agent told him the door was kept shut – not locked, but shut. The Almaric family didn't go in here.'

Hugo ran his hand down the wall by the door. 'This is the room we start in – painting it white. Then two of the bedrooms. Two have already been done, including the one we're in. There's a few acres of land and several outhouses to the side of the property, but we're to ignore those.'

He left the room and made for the stairs. The same thinning carpet from the hall continued up the middle of the black-painted staircase. Barley-twist spindles ran up to the banister at six-inch intervals. Alice felt the carved ridge of the rail under her hand as she ascended behind her boyfriend, noting the black was worn down to blond wood in places where the hands of almost 200 years, people long dead, had grasped it to walk up safely, just as she was today.

Rounding the bend at the top, there was a lofty window with a seat ledge to the left. Along the landing were a bathroom and three bedrooms, one being their own, another being empty while the third and largest had a four-poster with drapes tethered to the poles and a door leading to a little ensuite. 'This was the dressing room,' said Hugo, pointing to the small bathroom. 'It even had a hip bath in there when dad bought the place.'

Up a second flight of stairs, this time with plain spindles and a bare banister, were two further, smaller rooms with low ceilings and windows overlooking the back garden. 'I can't get my head around people having servants,' said Alice, enjoying the view over empty fields. 'Yet I'm guessing these were built for them?'

'Guess so. We're to decorate just one of these if we have time. Don't lean on the glass like that, sweetheart. The window frame is rotten.'

They pattered back down the creaking stairs, Alice enjoying the feel of the moulded handrail as it slid under her palm.

In the rear room, dust sheets covering the floorboards and marble fireplace, curtains down and folded in the hall, radio blaring, the couple painted in silence, Alice up the ladder daubing the picture rails while Hugo knelt to tackle the skirting.

Hugo was active, not passive like her last boyfriend, thought Alice as she watched him smooth paint along the wood. He'd organised their break and payment by his dad, sorted the train tickets, found the shop they'd got the cab to. Humming to the Bon Jovi song on the radio, she climbed down the ladder and dragged it in front of the window so she could paint the top of the frame. This guy was take-charge but not controlling, she mused, reaching high with her brush. Then she was falling, falling into space, one leg entangled in the ladder side rail. Managing to free her calf, she landed heavily on the other foot before ending up on her behind with a yelp as the ladder toppled to one side.

Hugo dropped his brush and leaped up. 'Babe! I've got you!' he cried, grasping Alice's elbow to pull her to her feet. Her heel pressed down a floorboard in front of the window, the end of which rose in the air with a squeak. 'Are you OK?'

'The floorboard nails were loose and it's gone up like a seesaw,' she giggled. 'My foot's gone in!' She stood, lifted her foot from the gap and rubbed her buttock. 'Can I be pervy and say I'll do that for you?' said Hugo, patting her bottom suggestively as she grinned and caught his hand.

Old-fashioned nails protruded from underneath the elevated board as Hugo examined it. 'No damage done. I'll dig around in the shed for a hammer.'

'Not till you've rubbed my bottom better!' murmured Alice, kissing him. Then she stopped, looking over his shoulder at the space where her foot had been. Light from the window glanced off something metallic. 'Hey.' She stooped over the space. 'What's that?'

Hugo hunkered down and swiped aside a dingy cloth which had once been yellow, scattering a family of startled woodlice. 'A metal box,' he exclaimed, lifting it out. 'Buried treasure, maybe? A last will and testament, leaving whoever owns the house a vault of gold bullion?'

'Most likely a few old letters and some dead insects,'

said Alice, but her eyes widened with interest.

They both sat back, the box between them on the floor. About 10 inches long, it was painted black, criss-crossed with scratches showing the silver of the metal through, with a thick brass handle on the top and a slender handle at either end. 'Locked, just to annoy us,' said Alice, attempting to lift the lid.

Hugo rose. 'Stay here. There's some WD-40 under the sink and we have that screwdriver we used to open the paint tins. It's our duty, as nosey parkers, to have a go at getting it open.'

He left the room. Alice sat looking at the box and slid a finger around the enamelled gold band that ran all the way around the lid face. Then she whipped her hand away.

She'd felt movement, almost imperceptible but definitely there, under her fingertip from inside the tin.

As she wondered if she'd imagined it, Hugo returned with the lubricant, stooping to snatch up the screwdriver on his way over to her. He picked up the box and shook it. Something rattled inside. 'Ooo! Treasure indeed! Right, my beauty, let's see if we can prise you open!' Placing it face down, he sprayed the hinges with lubricant, then worked the screwdriver in between the lid and box. 'Heave ho!'

The lid began to loosen, so Alice put the box the right way up. 'The great unveiling! Bagsy I lift the lid!'

Inside were six long, slim mottled structures, whitish yellow with dung-coloured patches of discolouration, thick at one end and tapered at the other. Hugo held his nose. 'What on earth are those? They smell like rotten – ugh, I don't know. Bad cooking fat? And they look like giant severed fingers.'

Alice laughed, taking one out. 'They're candles. Look, they have wicks. They are a *bit* stinky – don't exaggerate! I spotted candlesticks in the parlour and we have matches. We can have a romantic candlelit dinner. Or add to the atmosphere when we light the parlour fire. Which we are definitely going to do as part of our romantic getaway,' she added firmly. 'I bet they're original Victorian candles.'

'But why were they hidden under the floorboards in what looks like a cashbox?' mused Hugo.

'Given that whoever put them there wasn't thoughtful enough to leave a note, we'll never know,' said Alice. 'Let's get back to work. I'll pop these in the kitchen while you replace the floorboard.'

Holding the box steady, she took the candles through. Did they roll together longer than was strictly possible in the box when she set it down on the old, scrubbed table?

Maybe not...

They went back to their decorating and, mid-afternoon, Alice glanced at her paint-spattered watch. 'After 2pm and we haven't had lunch,' she declared, rubbing the back of her neck. 'I'm aching from craning backwards rollering the ceiling. You know what? I've got an urge for beans on toast, dirty beans on toast with thick slices of white bread spread with loads of butter and washed down with a big mug of builder's tea. We need more food anyway, so I'll get down to that village shop.'

'Yep, great,' said Hugo. 'I'll carry on with the decorating.'

It was spitting out, so Alice took a plastic bag and shrugged on her coat, slipping her purse in the pocket.

'Use the back door,' called Hugo. 'We can keep it open. No one will come in.' Alice grabbed an umbrella she'd found in a cupboard, an old black, dusty thing with a handle that looked suspiciously like bone and left the house through the glass-panelled rear door.

She crunched down the straight gravel path, noting the swathes of grass either side bordered by a low privet hedge, enjoying the peace and the scent of wet grass. At the end was a gap in the hedge rather than a gate, which she stepped through onto the lane. Her hood was sufficient protection against the thin drizzle, so she used the long umbrella as a walking stick to keep upright on the muddy lane.

It was icy, so she walked to the store as quickly as she could. Inside, Alice marched up to the counter, stamping her grimy boots on the flattened cardboard boxes spread around the floor for such a purpose. This time it was just the buttery-haired girl, whose elfin face and plump, pink cheeks made her look like a young teenager. The girl put down the magazine she was reading, her firm, confident stare and the way she looked Alice up and down with an air of mild distaste showing her to be 19 or 20.

'Yes?' she said brusquely. Undaunted by her

insolence, Alice took her time getting out her shopping list and unfolding it.

'Um... two tins of baked beans, a packet of unsmoked bacon, two pints of semi-skimmed milk and a thick white sliced loaf.'

'Milk and bacon in the fridge behind you,' said the girl, turning to get the other items.

As she rang up the food on her till, the girl said, not meeting Alice's eyes, 'So how are you getting on in the doctor's house?'

'Good,' said Alice. 'It's big and still needs quite a bit of work. But yeah, we're happy.' Then she decided to ask the question that had been on her mind ever since they'd been in the shop yesterday. The reason she'd wanted to come without Hugo. 'You said something about the doctor who built the house being a wrong 'un. What did you mean?'

The girl looked up. 'Well, it's always the same with you rich people,' she began.

'I'm not rich,' said Alice indignantly. 'Dr Gastrell's son is my boyfriend.'

'Yeah, well, doctors and the like. People with money and position. You take advantage of those not so fortunate. It was the same with him. Dr Clement.

'You seen his photo? No? I heard there's one in the house. He was a gentleman o' course, good-looking as well. He built that place as a family home but left his wife and kids in London most of the time. He'd come down on his own, so it would be just him and the servants, in particular the housekeeper. She had her own family, her husband down in the village, but Dr Clement was so demanding of her that she lived in a lot of the time. Caused no end of problems with her old man, it did.

'He would get her to do things – un-Christian things, although I'm not a believer.'

'What do you mean?' asked Alice, her mind conjuring up images of bizarre sexual practices. Her thoughts must have showed on her face as the girl laughed. 'No, not like that. Although he did take the housekeeper as his mistress. So they say.

'He was a surgeon, well respected, and he'd do some of his more – *unusual* medical experiments at the house. He'd get the housekeeper to help him in that big back room. So they say. I don't know exactly what went on, but the rumours were gross.'

'Tell me more about the rumours,' began Alice. The girl opened her mouth to continue but was interrupted by the tinny clang of the shop bell. A bedraggled woman in a headscarf came in holding a small boy by the hand. 'Want a comic and sweets,' he whined.

'It's a comic or sweets, but not both,' said the woman curtly, shaking the child's arm.

'Comic and sweets, comic and sweets!' came the thin wail, rising to a bawl.

Gathering her shopping, Alice took this as her cue to leave as the girl came out from behind the counter to mollify the child.

The rain had started up again and as Alice grappled with the huge umbrella on the shop doorstep, the girl opened the door at her back and stuck her head out. 'Cutting people,' she hissed, enjoying the look of surprise on Alice's face.

'What?'

'Cutting people up. That's what he did in the house. So they say.' The girl withdrew her head, slamming the door shut with a clang of the bell.

Alice set off down the lane, holding the heavy

umbrella at an angle to keep off the rain. What was she to make of this new information? She frowned. Surgeons certainly cut people up – that was their job. They were in the business of saving lives and she guessed surgical methods were basic and brutal in the 1800s. But why would a doctor be operating on people – if that's what the girl meant – in his own home? Maybe medics did that then?

Underfoot, the mud was looser than ever and once again, she passed the two graveyards at intervals. The one minutes from their property was the size of a school playground. How odd, she thought. Two so close together.

The house was ahead and Alice walked around the back, her coat brushing the wet leaves of the hedge on one side as she stepped through the gap into the garden. This was her first full view of the place from the rear and it looked even shabbier than at the front.

Coming towards the sludge-coloured building, the cement rendering dark with rain, she could see six windows, four like at the front plus the two attic windows. A movement caught her eye in the downstairs window of the room they were decorating.

Hugo had come to the sill and was looking out, his face milk-pale, dark hair swept away from his face. Beaming, Alice transferred the umbrella to the hand with the shopping and waved, breaking into a trot. Hugo remained motionless, gazing out past her. A few steps closer and she realised it wasn't Hugo. This face was more anaemic and it looked like a woman, a young woman. Letting her hand drop, she kept up her pace, hurrying towards the house. Then the face simply wasn't there anymore.

Reaching the back door, through the glass in the top panel she saw Hugo, swigging from a mug as he bent over a newspaper spread out on the table. She twisted the doorknob to let herself in. 'Have you come from the room we're decorating just this minute?'

Hugo looked up in surprise. 'Great to see you too. Pull that door to, gorgeous – you're letting the cold in. I've been sitting here warming my cockles, whatever they are, for the last 10 minutes. Why do you ask?'

'Oh, no reason,' said Alice turning away so as not to meet his eyes. 'Ready for beans on toast?'

Over their late lunch, Alice explained what the shop girl had told her about Dr Clement. 'I can't pretend to know a whole lot about Victorian surgeons,' began Hugo as he poured them more tea from a teapot they'd found. 'But you could loosely describe a surgeon's job as cutting people up – for their own benefit. And doctors had to practice their skills. Everyone knows there was a roaring trade in bodysnatching going on then – Burke and Hare and all that.'

Alice was cross. 'Here you go again, Hugo, making assumptions. I haven't grown up around doctors like you, nor did I study the sciences like you did, Mr I - P l a n n e d - T o - B e c o m e - A Doctor-But-Changed-My-Mind-After-A-Year-of-Medical-School. So tell me. About bodysnatching. Not too graphic, though – you'll put me off my beans.'

'Sorry.' Hugo looked crestfallen.

See, thought Alice. Sweet. Not like his dad at all.

'In the 1800s,' said Hugo, putting more bread in the toaster, 'medicine was advancing rapidly and students needed cadavers to dissect for anatomy tuition. Bodies came from the gallows, because part of a murderer's punishment was to end up on the dissecting table. But as more medics were training, there weren't enough corpses to go around, so we got the resurrectionists, or grave robbers, which meant no buried body was safe. It was inevitable that someone would start killing for cash, and the most famous killers were William Burke and William Hare, an enterprising pair who murdered people at Hare's Edinburgh boarding house and sold their corpses to the medical school. They were caught, Burke was hanged and, appropriately enough, wound up being dissected by docs himself.'

Hugo's eyes gleamed. 'Apparently at Burke's dissection, there was so much blood it cascaded across the floor, causing the students to slip.'

Alice stopped buttering toast and held up her hand. 'That's enough! How disgusting. This was in big towns, though. Not tiny villages. Presumably Dr Clement couldn't just start dissecting people wherever he fancied? Bringing his work home?'

'I doubt it,' said Hugo, sitting down with his plate. 'You know what people are like, with nothing better to do than gossip, especially somewhere small with not much going on. Maybe the locals were bitter about him having money and social standing–'

'And exploiting his housekeeper, ruining her fa
life,' finished Alice. 'Doctors' arrogance. We've see.
before...'

Now it was Hugo's turn to get cross. 'I've already
told you. Dad did not sexually assault that patient and
the hearing proved it. Yes, he has patients who fancy
him but he does nothing to encourage them.'

Alice couldn't stop herself. 'If it's rubbish, then why
has your mum whisked Anna and Peter away to her
parents' without a word? They're even going to school
from there.' Alice knew Hugo's mother was stiff and
formal with him on the phone these days, as he'd come
away from their calls downcast. Did Hugo's mum feel
her oldest son had to pick a side – and had chosen his
dad's?

The couple were glaring at each other when there
was a sudden crash to the side of them. On the floor in
front of the dresser lay the metal candle box. 'I moved
that to the top of the dresser from the table earlier,'
said Hugo, rising to put it back. 'I must have left it
close to the edge, so it fell off. What a racket it made
on the stone flags!'

Smiling at him, Alice felt unsettled. She'd put a tin

of beans by the box when she came in from shopping. Both had been several inches from the edge of the dresser.

Darkness was falling by the time they'd finished the first coats of paint in the back room. The pair chatted as they swirled the emulsion from their brushes down the sink, when Alice exclaimed, 'Shiiiit! It's Caroline's birthday today and I forgot to send her a card, let alone a present, what with the excitement of sorting out coming down here. I'll nip upstairs to the main bedroom to give her a call. Don't worry, I'm not going to talk about you!'

'Tell her hello from me,' said Hugo, reaching for the washing-up liquid.

After drying her hands on a tea towel, Alice ran lightly up the stairs and turned into the back bedroom, switching on the overhead light. The curtains were open and she could see the inky night sky outside. She still hadn't a clue where the nearest neighbours were, having passed no houses on the journey from the shop. The countryside was so dark, with not a streetlamp in sight. Ahead, the large window looked black as she sat down on the four poster's embroidered coverlet next the side table containing the phone and dialled her friend's number. It was picked up after three rings.

'Caro!' said Alice. 'Happy, happy birthday! Sorry about the card. Please say I'm still your bestie!'

Her friend gave a fruity chuckle. 'Yes, I still love you. I'll just about forgive you, knowing this is your make-or-break fortnight with Mr Arrogant.'

'Shush! It's going pretty well so far but it has only been two days,' she whispered. 'I'll share all when I'm back – I'm sure there'll be loads to tell you!

'What are you doing for your birthday?' she continued at her normal volume.

They chatted about Caro's evening plans. 'How's the job hunt going?' enquired Alice. Caroline had also worked at the magazine and lost her job and was staying with her mother while she got back on her feet.

'You know,' she replied, 'I'm enjoying working in Mum's second-hand bookshop more than I thought I would...'

'Antiquarian,' Alice corrected. 'Your mum would chuck you straight out if she heard you call it that!'

'True. Anyway, I enjoy selling books but I couldn't

work with Mum full time – she's too intense. I'll get some more experience, then approach one of the big bookstores. Any more thoughts what you'll do jobwise when you get back to London? You have rent to pay and birthday girls to treat!'

'I've faxed off applications for a handful of magazine posts – there's plenty of work, so I'll be fine.'

The doorbell rang out at Caroline's end. 'Must dash – the girls are here. We'll toast you!'

'Happy birthday again,' sang Alice, replacing the receiver.

The instant she put it in its cradle, the lights went out, plunging her in darkness so total it was as though someone had wrapped a black velvet cloth around her eyes. A storm whipped up outside, rain hitting the window with a rattle that sounded like handfuls of gravel being thrown against the glass.

With a gasp, Alice got to her feet, the large room so unfamiliar it was surprisingly difficult to find her way to the door.

Footsteps, far away. Then mounting the stairs from the bottom. Slowly.

'Hugo?' she called.

Silence greeted her, except for the footsteps, which continued to walk deliberately up the stairs to the top. Lightning flashed through the window and, in that moment, illuminated a figure in the doorway. A woman – white face, scraped-back hair, a black slash instead of a mouth. Another flash of lightening and the space was empty.

A bang came from the floor beneath her. The back door slamming? Then Hugo's voice, coming closer.

'Alice?' Heavy steps thumped up the stairs. 'I was in the garden taking the paint pots outside when all the lights went out. You still in the bedroom?'

Now it was Hugo revealed in the flash of lightning in the doorway. Seeing Alice standing wide-eyed with shock by the bed, he rushed forward to hold her. 'The lights have fused, that's all. Did you do something that might have caused it?'

Relieved, she put her arms around his neck. 'I don't think so, although they went off the second I put the receiver down.'

She could tell from Hugo's voice that he was frowning. 'I doubt it would be that. The phone is on a different electric circuit from the rest of the house in case people need to call the emergency services or whatever.'

He led her out of the room. 'Let's light some candles and look for the fuse box. A bulb has probably blown somewhere in the house and that will have triggered the fuse to cut out. It's simply a case of flicking back up the switch that's gone down, then we can find the dead bulb.'

The couple walked carefully down the stairs in the dark and headed for the kitchen. Another streak of lightening showed them the dresser with the box of candles. Thankfully, a sliver of moon peeped through the clouds at the window, offering some illumination. Opening the metal box, Alice took out two candles while Hugo ferreted in the kitchen drawer for matches. 'We can take one each into the parlour and slot it into a candlestick,' he said.

Hugo struck a match, applied it to the wicks and took one from her. 'This feels greasier than you'd expect,' he said. 'Slimy.' Their faces glowed yellow in the small circles of light. 'They don't give out much light.'

In the parlour, they approached the round table and

placed a candle in each of the two candlesticks in the middle. Alice wrinkled her nose. 'Euw! They really do stink! What does that smell remind you of?'

Hugo pulled a face in the gloom. 'Rancid meat – rotten, fatty meat. So rotten I could throw up. And there's black smoke trailing out of them.'

'That's it,' said Alice. 'Bad meat. Let's find the fuse box quick so we can blow these horrors out. They're dripping madly, too.' The fatty substance melted fast and was oozing down the candlesticks. Coughing at the smoke, they headed for the cupboard under the stairs, Alice bearing one candle. 'Fuse boxes are normally here, aren't they?' Hooking her finger under the old-fashioned catch, she pulled. And pulled. 'It's stuck. You have a go.'

Hugo couldn't budge the latch either. 'It's like it's nailed shut. Where's that screwdriver?' Alice waited by the door as he went to the back room for it. Feeling a slight ruffling of the hair at the back of her neck, she turned.

The woman again, eyes fixed on hers. This time Alice screamed, long and high. Hugo sprinted over, his face creased with concern in the dim light.

'What...'

'There's a woman here. Young, in a long dress, with your colouring. This is the third time I've seen her. And she's not real.'

Hugo gawped. 'The third time...?' Alice described spotting the woman at the back window, and then upstairs when the lights went off. To her annoyance, Hugo's lips began to twitch as he suppressed a smile. 'And she was here just now?'

Alice gazed over his shoulder and started. 'She's still here...' He whirled around as the woman stepped into the shadows by the wall, melting into them.

'Don't tell me – I scared her off!' He chuckled, jamming the screwdriver under the latch. 'Let's get the power back on. That will get rid of her for good.'

The door refused to budge, even after Hugo planted two kicks squarely on the latch with his heel. 'Jesus!' he said angrily. 'And I'm suffocating with these disgusting candles.'

'Disgusting, but we need them,' said Alice, subdued. 'And they don't last long – both are almost finished. The wicks don't burn away like normal candles. Fetch the scissors so we can chop off the spent wick or they'll go out. I'm searching the kitchen for normal ones that don't make me want to bring up my beans. Looks like we're stuck with candles for now.'

Positioning the candlesticks with their stinky cargo on the kitchen table, the couple rummaged in the kitchen drawers and under the sink, to no avail. 'I'll check the dresser drawers,' said Alice. There were three deep ones in a row, which she slid open in turn. 'Nope. Nope. Nope... but what's this?'

In the last drawer lay a flat, rectangular object. It was a photograph, an oval in the centre of a silver-coloured metal frame. 'Judging from the clothes, this must be the Great Man, although there's no name I can see,' she said, holding it up. 'The girl at the shop thought the doc's picture was here somewhere. Look at that arrogant stare! Not a man you'd argue with.'

Aged around 35, the man had a lofty brow with wavy hair swept to one side, his firm jaw almost hidden by a stiff white collar and elaborately arranged black necktie. 'He's holding a book, to emphasise the fact he's an educated man,' said Hugo, coming to look. 'What a handsome devil – look at those sensuous lips. Not sure about the fluffy mutton chops though.'

Alice wasn't in the mood for levity, so she replaced the photo and closed the drawer. 'Where were we? Stuck with just candles?'

Hugo shrugged. 'Specifically, stuck with *these* candles.' He opened the metal box. 'And we only have four left, so let's take one at a time.'

Alice felt alarmed. 'That means we'll have to go everywhere together or one of us will be stranded in the dark.' One candle had gone out and she watched fearfully as Hugo lit a third from the smouldering wick of the remaining one. 'It's freezing without the heating. Given that it's only 7pm, we have a lot of cold and darkness to get through before we can call an electrician in the morning.'

'Which is Sunday,' Hugo reminded her. 'I can't see us finding help until Monday. Not in this place.'

'We could light a fire,' said Alice.

'Gosh, yes, the romantic fire you wanted!'

Not so romantic now, thought Alice. More to keep the ghosts and shadows at bay.

Hugo made an exasperated sound. 'We have newspaper to start it off, but nothing for fuel, short of smashing up one of Dad's antique chairs.'

Alice clutched his arm. 'Your dad! Call him and ask where the fuse box is! And whether there's firewood or coal...'

'Or if we can smash up a chair?' Hugo gave a wry smile. 'Way ahead of you. I thought of that. But look.' He took out his diary and showed it her. 'Dad, Madeira,' he read. 'Phone number: as you can see, the ink ran when my rucksack got wet. The number's illegible and I never asked him the name of the hotel.'

'Call your mother then. She must have his number? In case there's an emergency with the kids?'

'Have you forgotten? Her parents have just moved house – and I don't have their new number.'

Sitting down, Alice said, 'OK. Let's be rational. The village shop should be open tomorrow. They'll have candles and maybe wood for the fire. And the woman said her Walter worked on the house. She'll be able to help us with the dead fuses.'

With no electricity, they couldn't even heat soup or a kettle on the electric hob, so they opted for bread and cheese at the table, Alice all the while watching the shadows for the woman, shoulders hunched to her ears with tension. The stone flags were cold underfoot even through their trainers and they could see their breath in the air.

'I give up,' said Hugo, standing up to brush the remains of his sandwich into the bin. 'This stench has killed my appetite. Let's go to bed and talk. At least we can get warm under the covers.'

Alice led the way up the stairs, shading the candle with her hand and averting her eyes as they passed the open doorway of the master bedroom.

In their room, they didn't undress for bed and went to the bathroom together to clean their teeth and use the loo, each waiting in the doorway as the other took their turn on the pan. 'In two months we've already adopted the habits of an old married couple,' joked Hugo. Alice didn't feel like laughing and she shivered in front of the mirror, baring her toothpaste-frothed teeth at herself.

Their room had looked inviting last night in the gleam of the side lamps. Tonight, in the light of the one candle on the bedside table, rather than lending Hugo's features a flattering, romantic glow, Alice thought he looked too perfect, almost other-worldly handsome. Like his father. They settled into bed, Hugo on his back with his arms tight around her, her head on his chest. Rather than feel safe, she felt like his captive.

Alice listened to the music of his words rather than the meaning, murmuring, 'Um-hum' every now and then to make out she was taking them in. But really, she was listening to the room. To the house.

The word 'career' caught her attention. 'Hugo?' she interrupted. 'You never told me why you left medical school. Why you didn't become a doctor, like your dad wanted.'

Her boyfriend let out a long sigh that warmed the crown of her head. 'It wasn't just me following in Dad's footsteps like I had no will of my own. I genuinely wanted to do the job when I was a teenager. But as I matured a bit, I saw how tough his work made Mum's life – he was always at the hospital, his patients came first and it seems we were too fit and healthy to interest him.' Hugo snorted. 'I saw the toll it takes on your family and I don't want that. I want to be around for my wife and kids. Not be an absent but loaded father who thinks he can make up for never being home by throwing bikes and other expensive stuff at his family. Yes, Mum has two diamond necklaces, but she often didn't get to see her husband for their wedding anniversary.

'Another problem was the dissections.' He paused.

'The dissections?' echoed Alice as encouragement for him to continue.

She felt his form shift beneath her, as though he felt uncomfortable talking about this. 'Not all med schools do full-body dissections. At some, you simply watch the lecturer do them. But at mine, we were expected to do our own. You'd have the dead person there – a corpse. And you'd have to take a scalpel and cut into their skin. Into human flesh.' Hugo sighed again. 'I'd take the scalpel, and I'd hold my breath, but I couldn't make a cut. It's such a deep-rooted taboo, not to cut into human flesh. I just couldn't overcome it. So I left.' He kissed her forehead. 'I know I joked about dissection earlier. That old public-school bravado. But it's not for me.

'After that term, I asked Dad how he did it. How, as a neurosurgeon, he can plunge a scalpel into another human being and slice them open. "Because

I'm detached from them," he told me. "I have no emotional link to patients. But I couldn't operate on you, or your mum, or Anna and Peter. I wouldn't have that distance." How ironic. He certainly feels distant from the family to me.'

There's a theme of doctors treating others like objects, thought Alice. He continued to speak and her mind began to wander again. A catch in Hugo's voice made Alice want to slither up the bed to kiss him, but then she froze. In front of her, close by the bed, was the woman. Hugo's eyes must be shut as he gave no sign of having seen her.

Out of the covers, Alice's cheeks felt chilled by the air emanating from the figure, cold as if from the grave, buried deep down in the freezing ground. Alice felt her body stiffen, but, opening her mouth, no sound came out.

Feeling her grow rigid in his arms, Hugo gave Alice's upper body a squeeze. 'Sweetheart, what–' he began, then gasped as he opened his eyes. This time, Alice noticed the woman was dressed in a white, floor-length garment, presumably a shroud. Her arms hung limply by her sides and Alice could make out dark patches across the woman's ribcage. She was mouthing words through her blackened lips, a pleading expression on her blanched face.

'W-what's she saying?' whispered Hugo. The woman's pleading became more urgent, desperate. Then, like a hologram switching images, they saw the apparition from behind, although she hadn't moved position. Ebony hair piled on her head, the upper back of her garment stained dark over a wide area. Her front was towards them again and she leaned into Alice's face, shrivelled lips moving rapidly as she tried to make herself understood.

Suddenly the candle snuffed out, leaving them in total blackness. This time the yell came from Hugo. Alice heard him scrabbling frantically on the side for the matches to light the fourth candle they'd brought up. What seemed like long minutes passed before a sickly light shone on the bed once more. They were alone.

Ashen-faced, Hugo said, 'What can I say? I'm sorry I doubted you.'

Trembling, Alice climbed out of bed, dragging the quilt off. 'Grab the pillows. We're going to the parlour to light the fire and I'm afraid we're going to smash up as many chairs as it takes to keep it lit until morning. I don't care what your dad thinks. He's sunning himself on a beach while we're dealing with... well, I don't know what but it's not good.'

Kneeling in front of the fireplace, they worked together, Alice twisting lengths of newspaper and laying them in the grate while Hugo balanced three turned chair legs and part of a frame on the top. 'What did she want, do you think, our spirit?' he asked. 'I can't believe we're even having this conversation.'

'I couldn't read her withered lips. I don't know. Hopefully she won't bother to come back to enlighten us.' Yet Alice knew she would.

Hugo held a match to the paper, then rose as it caught fire. 'There's a set of fire irons there. Get the poker and give the fire a prod while I run to fetch candle number five.'

Having something to do made Alice feel a little calmer. She prodded at the chair legs and wondered if they should have broken them up when–

'Argh!' A loud crash came from the kitchen, followed by Hugo's yelp.

Jumping to her feet, Alice left the glow of the firelight and raced down the shadowed hall. As she reached the kitchen door, she caught a glimpse of Hugo sitting on the floor in the moonlight clutching his foot, face contorted in pain – then the door banged shut in her face.

The only light came from the parlour fire through the open door several yards behind her. The storm had died down and the rain had been unobtrusive during the past hour, or maybe it was more that they'd been so distracted they'd ceased to notice it.

Now the wind whistled under the front door next to her, rain pattering on the wood. Her hand on the kitchen doorknob, she could hear Hugo calling her name from behind the door, but a rushing in her ears drowned him out. Cold air swirled around her face and what felt like wet fingers fluttered across her forehead. A woman's voice seemed all around her and, although she didn't want to let the words through, she heard, '*Burree... burree... burree...*' Releasing the doorknob, Alice clamped sweating palms over her ears, shaking her head to clear it of the keening voice.

In her mouth was the copper taste of blood. Alice

had bitten her tongue in fright. Then the swirling cold stopped.

The kitchen door creaked open. Moonlight revealed Hugo on the floor massaging his foot, sock dangling from his toes. 'I've been calling you – where did you get to? That damn cashbox–' It was open beside him face down, the last candle having rolled under the table.

Alice helped him into a chair. 'I went to pick up the box and it actually jumped off the shelf and landed on my foot,' he said, face grim. 'I think it's broken – it smashed hard into the top of my foot. Ow!' he exclaimed, when Alice touched the flesh gently.

'It's already swelling,' she said. 'Hopefully it's only bruised. Let's see if your dad keeps frozen peas in the freezer – or should I say, half-frozen peas, given that there's been no electricity for a few hours.'

Crossing the room, her foot collided with the upturned cashbox, sliding it a few inches across the tiles. A dull clang came from inside it. Alice bent down and lifted the box, releasing a sheet of metal which fell out and landed noisily on the floor, followed by a light, rectangular object.

'Hey! The jolt of hitting the floor – sorry, your foot – dislodged a panel in the box. And there was something stuck behind it.'

Hugo groaned. 'Alice, I'm in agony here. Get me the peas – and find some painkillers. I've had more than enough of that box. I don't care if it's got the crown jewels hidden in it.'

A rapidly defrosting bag of peas and a bottle of paracetamol – she didn't dare check the use-by date – meant Hugo allowed Alice to support him into the parlour, arm around her neck as he limped painfully by her side. Settling him in a chair by the fire, Alice propped his foot on a stool, made him comfortable and put the rest of the broken-up chair on the fire along with a wooden hedgehog ornament. It blazed brightly.

Leaving the door wide to allow as much light as possible into the hall, she carried the candle to the kitchen, collecting the spare one and the item from the box.

Back in the parlour, she closed the door to keep in the heat and light, manoeuvred a winged armchair close to Hugo and set a side table between them with the candle. 'I'm so used to the oily stink of those things that I no longer care,' she said. 'I'm just grateful we have them. That should be "had them". There's only one left.'

Hugo stared at his foot, ignoring her. 'It's almost twice the size. And turning purple. At least the painkillers are having some effect.' He exhaled impatiently. 'Anyway, let's look at your find.'

Leaning towards him into the pool of candlelight, she held it out. A small book, bound in brown leather. On seeing it, Hugo seemed to start before composing himself, an unreadable expression on his face. Slightly bewildered by this, Alice opened it at the front. 'It's not a printed book. This is a notebook, with handwriting in pencil.' Whoever had written in it was heavy-handed, pressing the pencil so hard it had almost dug through the yellowing pages.

Hugo threw his head back and laughed, despite his foot. 'Don't tell me. It's by the doctor and it's like one Frankenstein might have left behind, entitled *The Secret Of My Success.*'

'I thought you of all people might find this interesting. And we have no real idea what Dr

Clement got up to, or even whether this had anything to do with him.' Silently, Alice flicked through the pages. 'First couple are blank, as you might expect. Then the third page reads, "Cutis vera Josephine Fernsby, 1855". There aren't many pages, but the rest are stuck together, so we can't go any further. What does *cutis vera* mean? Is that Latin? Didn't you study that at your public school, posh boy?'

'It was on offer, but I'm not one for dead languages,' said Hugo. 'Latin was a requirement for med school up until the Sixties, so I didn't need it to get in. I did German, *meine Liebe*.

'So, a smattering of Latin and a woman's name? Maybe Josephine Fernsby was the housekeeper and this is hers.' He took the book from her, turning it over to examine the back before inspecting the writing inside. 'Although I don't know how educated she might have been. This writing is neat and ordered.'

'Maybe *she* was neat and ordered – and literate,' replied Alice. The fire suddenly flared bright in the centre as the wicker chair seat collapsed in a rush of crackling sparks, making them both jump.

'So is Josephine Fernsby, possible housekeeper, our

ghost?' asked Alice, yawning.

'There is no ghost,' said Hugo, rubbing his eyes, the book on his lap. 'I'd sell my soul for a cup of tea. Not to mention some sleep. Did you know it's past 4am?'

Alice snatched the book off him, sitting up straight. 'You saw her! And I heard her, in the hall when you got hurt and the kitchen door banged shut. She spoke to me.'

Hugo closed his eyes. 'I hope you said, "Not tonight, Josephine" in reply. Chuck me that quilt?'

'Don't dismiss me,' said Alice quietly.

'Sorry. It's been a long night. What did your ghost say?'

'I'm not sure, but she kept repeating something like, "Burree."'

'Here's what I think,' said Hugo, taking her hand and pressing it against his cheek. 'We got into bed and were half asleep, not to mention half-suffocated from trying to breathe without taking in too much of that candle pong. You said, "There's a woman by the bed" and autosuggestion led me to see what you described. Plus,' – he kissed the back of her hand and gazed into her eyes – 'this is a new relationship, two months in, and we're both still on our best behaviour trying to impress the other. At least, I am.' He grinned. 'It's stressful, not being able to just be ourselves. And we're both worried about getting a new job. So we're both under strain, with our imaginations running riot in a spooky old house with no lights.'

Patting her hand, he put it down with a smile. 'Give us a kiss.' She leaned in to meet his lips with hers. 'Why not pull your chair right up close to mine, grab that quilt and tuck it around us, and let's get some sleep. It'll be light soon, then we can sort all this out. Leave the book on the table.'

Alice did as he asked, bringing over a tartan rug. She felt troubled. Leaning her head against the chair wing, she shut her eyes.

Upstairs, she hadn't mentioned there being a woman close to the bed.

Weak daylight streamed in through the window when Alice awoke, stiff from her hours in the chair. Ahead, the fire was down to a handful of glowing embers. On the chair beside her, Hugo slumbered on, his normally carefully arranged hair falling over his forehead, pursed pink lips emitting regular puffs of breath. He was difficult, he was stroppy, he was childish at times, but she did have strong feelings for him. Whether those feelings were strong enough to carry them all the way to the altar, she had yet to discover.

Stretching her arms above her head and legs out in front of her, she eased her muscles so they'd do her bidding and got up, slipping the rug from Hugo's knees and draping it over her shoulders. It was nearly 8am by her watch.

The hall and staircase looked innocent enough in the daylight, so she climbed the steps to wash her face and brush her teeth in the bathroom. In the kitchen, she poured milk and cereal, leaving Hugo to sleep.

At 8.30am, she stuck her head around the parlour door. Hugo snoozed on. May as well go to the shop for firewood and proper candles, she thought, plus she could ask if the shop woman knew an electrician.

Minutes later, she was trudging down the lane, a church bell pealing nearby. Ah yes, of course – it was Sunday. Would people be in church? Alice hadn't seen one, but then again she and Hugo hadn't explored any of the village bar the road from the shop.

A sign in the shop window announced Sunday opening hours to be 9am to 3pm. It was 8.50am and Alice stood outside, hands thrust in her coat pockets as she stamped her feet, to keep warm as well as through impatience.

At 9.15am, the woman ambled from the back of the shop brandishing a key and Alice resisted the temptation to tap her watch and announce, 'You're quarter of an hour behind schedule! Such inefficiency!'

'You look rough, duck, if you don't mind me saying,' said the woman, standing back to let her in. Alice wasn't sure if she detected sympathy or amusement in the woman's tone, so chose to ignore this, instead asking for candles and firewood.

'Candles we got,' said the woman, 'but the wood bundle is heavy. You've got radiators – why do you want wood? Ah,' she said with a wink. 'Romantic fire. Got you. I can get some sent over.'

Once again astounded by the woman's rudeness and overfamiliarity, Alice said tightly, 'Our electrics blew last night, in the storm. They obviously hadn't been installed properly. That means we have no lights and no heating, because the gas boiler needs electricity to work. The other day, you mentioned someone who'd worked on the house? Might he be able to help?'

The woman began roaring with laughter, then checked herself. 'My husband Walter did the electrics and he'd have done them perfect. I shouldn't laugh. You must have been brass monkeys last night. Walter?' She turned and shouted his name over her shoulder through the open door. 'Walter!'

A small man with a thick grey moustache like a scrubbing brush and deep lines leading from his nose to his down-turned mouth appeared behind her. The woman nodded in Alice's direction and said, 'This young lady's from the doctor's house.' Walter raised his eyebrows, indicating that his wife had already filled him in on the couple. 'The electrics blew last night and they have no heating or lights. You don't normally work Sundays, but we can't leave them till tomorrow. Not in this weather.'

'Oh no, we can't have that,' said Walter. 'I'll fetch

the van round the front, give you a lift. No charge.'

Sitting next to Walter in the vehicle, a bag of wood on her knees, Alice listened as he talked, not asking questions, which she was grateful for, but supplying a string of anecdotes about Nathwaite Corner.

'The doctor what built it, we still talk about him now, even though it were what, nearly 130 year ago when he died. At first, the village people were pleased he'd moved here – famous doctor from London, used his money to build the church and a couple of graveyards. And when he was home, he'd tend to the locals when they were sick. His servants were very loyal to him, particularly the housekeeper.'

'Josephine Fernsby?' cut in Alice. 'Was that the housekeeper?

Walter, who had been calm and measured so far, turned to look at her. 'No. The housekeeper was Mrs Tucker. Where d'you hear that name?'

'I-I-er, I'm not sure,' stammered Alice.

They passed the last churchyard, the one closest to Nathwaite Corner. 'That doctor wronged Josephine Fernsby,' he growled. 'Her grave's in there.'

Walter parked his van in front of the house, his

chatty demeanour gone. 'Yes, that's where I saw the name. In the churchyard,' lied Alice.

Briefly glancing her way, Walter strode along the path, Alice hurrying to catch up. 'What did the doctor do to Josephine? I mean, how did he wrong her?'

He glared at her. 'Got the key? I have other business today.'

Fitting the key into the lock, Alice let Walter enter first. Goodness, she thought. If this was village life, she was staying in London forever.

Inside, Walter went straight to the cupboard under the stairs, opening the door with ease. Alice watched as he swung his flashlight in and located the fuse box. 'See, all these switches have the room they correspond to written on labels above them. The one to that big back room is down. That means the bulb has blown. The lightbulbs are here.' He pointed to a box in the corner, took one out and disappeared into the rear room. Moments later, he returned to the fuse box, flipped up the switch and lights flared all over the house. 'Easy when you know how,' he muttered and she was sure he said 'stupid townies' under his breath.

Thanking Walter, she saw him out and realised she'd

heard nothing from Hugo – in fact, the house was completely silent. Surely he wasn't still asleep? It was well after 10am.

Behind her, Alice heard the heating firing up. Even though they no longer needed the firewood, she carried a few logs in to the parlour.

The quilt sat heaped in the chair, the flaccid bag of peas wilting on the stool.

But no Hugo.

Panic rose in her chest and she placed a hand there to comfort herself, perching on the edge of Hugo's chair. He must be here somewhere – he could barely walk two steps without her last night. Surely he'd heard her come in with Walter?

It struck her that she didn't want to be alone in this house.

Leaving the wood in the hearth, she entered the hall, now warming up thanks to the radiators. No Hugo in the kitchen either. Maybe he was in the bathroom.

Cautiously, she took the stairs a step at a time. They creaked underfoot and as she reached the middle landing, she heard a voice, a man's, in the master bedroom. These doors were so heavy they muffled sounds behind them. Hugo was on the phone, that was it!

She pushed the door and Hugo was sat on the bed, back against the headboard, his sore foot stretched out in front. Seeing her, a look spread over his face that made her catch her breath. Guilt? Wariness? Alarm?

Bending his lips to the receiver, he said, 'Yeah. Certainly. Speak soon.'

Hugo gave a weak smile. 'That was Mum, making sure we were managing.'

Alice looked at him curiously. 'Did you ask for the number of your dad's hotel? We could do with it, in case we have any more emergencies.' His blank expression told her he hadn't. 'Did you get *her* number?'

'Er...'

'Was that even your mum on the line?'

'Who else would it be?' He peered beseechingly at her through his fringe, which he pushed back. 'My foot is still damn sore, but the swelling's gone down. I heard you downstairs with that workman.'

'Who opened the under-stairs cupboard with ease and fixed the electrics...'

'Excellent. Be a doll and run me a bath?' He groaned theatrically, then gave her a cheeky wink. 'Join me in there? It's a big bath.' He patted the bed beside him and Alice sat down. 'Mmmm... I love that you have that Pre-Raphaelite Lizzie Siddal thing going on with your copper hair,' he murmured, winding a fistful of her thick locks around his wrist and pulling her to him. 'Loose curls and looser morals driving innocent men like me and Dante Gabriel Rossetti mad with desire.' Reaching around, he pinched her backside hard. 'Not to mention this deliciously fat, sorry, luxurious ass.'

'Rude,' she admonished, getting to her feet, a mixture of desire and anger whirling around her breast. Alice's feelings towards Hugo were as up and down as a rollercoaster. Hugo said he loved her. Then he'd belittle her – 'It's in jest,' he'd assure her. 'At my boys' school, we ribbed each other mercilessly and it's hard to get out of the habit. I'm doing my best to though, for you.' He could be caring and kind, but why was he lying about who'd been on the phone? Another girl? And was he trying to distract her with talk of her looks...?

She pondered this as she turned the taps on in the bathroom. Could she trust him? Or should she return to London and give up on this relationship? Yet Hugo had so many of the qualities she'd been seeking in a guy and not found before. And she was ashamed to admit even to herself that the idea of becoming part of a well-off family was appealing, after growing up in a scruffy maisonette in Leeds with a mother who, after her last marriage failed, was so depressed she rarely left her bed. A mother who was drinking herself to death, deaf to Alice's entreaties to get help.

Swishing the water to mix the hot and cold, she thought about his family – the family she could be joining. Money, of course, didn't mean closeness. It sounded as though is mother lived a lonely life, all lunches with friends and shopping trips and there were few times when the whole family were together. At least Hugo was clear he wanted things to be different for the household he made.

Hugo hobbled in behind her naked and slipped into the water. Don't let that body make your decision for you, she told herself, taking up the soap and lathering his athletic chest with its tangle of black hair. He caught her wrist, grinning. 'In you get. We don't want you stinking like those candles, do we.'

'Oh, thanks,' she laughed, stripping off her jeans and top. Again, not a very nice thing to say...

At breakfast, she outlined her odd conversation with Walter.

'So Josephine Fernsby wasn't the housekeeper – she was some wench "wronged" by the good doctor,' said Hugo. 'Sounds like he ruined the virtue of at least two women if we count Mrs Tucker too. Busy boy. And a typical upper-class Victorian – do as I say, not as I do.'

Ignoring the levity of his tone so as to avoid an argument, Alice said, 'The weather's mild today and I can't believe that we haven't taken a look around the village yet. Do you fancy getting wrapped up and venturing out?'

Hugo inspected his foot. 'If I bundle this up with an extra sock and put my trainers on, I guess I'll be OK for 20 minutes if I take that umbrella-cum-walking stick.'

Suitably attired, they set off down the lane.

On the way back, Alice nodded at the cemetery nearest the house. 'Probably be a needle in a haystack, but let's look for Josephine's grave.'

Under her hand, the black iron gate opened with a creak of its hinges. The headstones protruded from the frozen ground, silent sentinels watching over the dead, the lettering on most worn to near illegibility by time and weather. Hefty-trunked, mature trees twitched their branches in the winter breeze, overhanging tombstones green with lichen. Some had chunks smashed off, while others leant drunkenly to one side.

Alice walked down the gravelled paths, occasionally stepping onto the grass for a closer look at a certain grave while Hugo made his way gingerly along behind her. To their left, a crow pecked at a pile of red berries under a holly bush, flapping away with an indignant screech as they approached.

After inspecting several dozen headstones, she exclaimed, 'Maybe it's not here. The wind is picking up and it's drizzling. I give up. Let's go before we end up soaked again. We're close to the exit anyway.'

'Yeah, and my foot's suddenly jolly sore,' said Hugo. 'Let me lean on you, sweetheart.' Alice took a few steps towards him and tripped over a clump of grass, landing on her hands and knees before a gravestone. 'Goodness!' she exclaimed, passing a gloved hand over the inscription. 'Here's our lady! Right by the gate. We walked past this when we came in, but we missed it because the gravestone is facing the other direction.

'Josephine Alice Fernsby – well, that middle name was unexpected,' she went on. 'Born 1837, died 1855. Only 18, poor love. I wonder what happened to the baby? If there was one. Plenty of people buried here – maybe he or she is too? Or wouldn't the child have been interred with her?'

'There was no baby. That's not what he did.' They both started as Walter came through the gate and stopped in front of them. He was hatless, heedless of the rain wetting his hair, which was getting heavier by the minute. His sudden appearance rendered Alice and Hugo speechless.

'It's not just me what hangs around graveyards on a Sunday, I see,' he said bitterly. 'I can't be doing with the hypocrisy of the church. The wife goes every week, and I go walking while our girl minds the shop. War, poverty, those with power lording it over the rest of us.' He stared pointedly at Hugo, who stared back. 'No God I can respect would allow those things.'

Given that Walter seemed in the mood to talk, Alice wanted him to keep going. 'What happened to Josephine?' she asked softly.

The man shrugged his collar up to his ears and stuck his hands in his pockets. 'Doctor cut her up. Dissected her like a common criminal. Lied to cover it up, he did.

'She got taken ill at home and died suddenly. Dr Clement was called, but she'd passed before he arrived. Told the family it was dangerous to keep her body in the house – this was when they had a theory that the dead gave off poisonous gases that could kill you. So he took her body back with him – still warm, she was – in his fancy carriage, said his housekeeper would lay Josephine out and he'd pay for the burial. The family were grateful.

'On the day of the funeral, the horses carried her to the grave, like he'd said. But clumsy beggars lifting the box dropped it, the lid came off and she slipped out. Josephine's face and hands were perfect. But her shroud ruckled up, showing holes in her belly and bloody great stitches on the rest of her. Took advantage for his own ends.

'But what could people do? He was a doctor. Folks gathered her up, put her in the box and she went underground.' Walter looked sad.

'Was this a relative of yours?' asked Hugo on a hunch.

'Aye. My great-great-gran's sister. I don't tell the tale nowadays. Even my wife doesn't know the details. It's shaming. That the family let it happen. Didn't have the power to stop him.

'As far as we know, he was embarrassed at being caught and confined his dissections to London after that. He wasn't called out to the village when folk were sick no more. Nor was he seen at the house as much. Used to do his nastiness in that back room and the Almarics shut it up. Said it had a bad atmosphere.'

The couple walked the few minutes home in silence. Hugo unlocked the rear door. 'Maybe Clement's interest in building the graveyards was somewhat, shall we say, predatory,' he said. 'Makes you wonder whether it was so he had easy access to fresh bodies to chop up or even sell on.'

Alice nodded. 'Nathwaite Corner? He should have called his house Cutting Corner. Or The Dissection Dwelling.' The phone was ringing in the hall and she rushed forward to grab the receiver.

'Caroline! Hi!'

'I'm calling to see how it's going with lover boy,' said her friend.

Should I tell her about our ghost, Alice wondered? Meanwhile, here was an opportunity to ask her about the book.

'Caro, we found a leather-bound notebook we think may have belonged to the doctor who built the house. According to the locals, he was a major oddball and he – or whoever it was – wrote something on the first page of the book I wanted to ask you about. Hang on, I'll get it.'

She put the receiver down and darted into the parlour for the volume. Flipping to the front, she said, 'It says "Cutis vera Josephine Fernsby". Any idea what cutis vera means?'

'No, but given it's to do with old books, Mum

might. I'll shout her – she's making lunch.' Alice heard Caroline exchange a few words with her mother, who came on the phone quickly, as though she'd snatched the receiver off her daughter.

'Hi, Alice,' came her clipped, tense voice. 'This is Susan. Do you have the book in front of you?'

'I do.'

'And do you have a good source of light?'

Moving closer to the hall window, Alice confirmed that she had.

'Describe the book. Colour? What's the grain like?'

'Tawny brown. Very fine grain, smooth, smoother than normal leather I'd say.'

Susan's next words made Alice's heart skip a beat.

'Roll your sleeve up and hold the book against the back of your wrist. Look carefully at the grain and compare it to your arm.'

Worried, Alice lodged the receiver between her ear and the crook of her shoulder as she looked from her arm to the book and back again. 'Sorry – what am I looking for?'

'Pay particular attention to the hair follicle pattern. I'd expect them to look similar – very similar. Cutis vera means "skin of". What's the rest of that phrase?'

Alice told her.

'It seems the writer is making it plain that the book is bound in the skin of Josephine Fernsby.'

Alice dropped the book on the phone table with a small cry.

'But – but that's barbaric. How can anyone cover a book in human flesh?'

'Using human skin to cover books is known as anthropodermic bibliopegy. I agree that nowadays it sounds like something only a serial killer would do. But back in the nineteenth century, that wasn't the case. Some doctors would have books bound in human skin from a dissection they'd carried out. There are several documented cases of them doing so, usually from an executed man who had been dissected in front of anatomy students.

'We don't know how many of these exist; only a handful have been verified. There is one bound in the skin of William Burke, the notorious murderer, in a Scottish museum. But you have a very rare book, and a collector would pay a hefty fee for it.'

That Burke guy again! Rather than sound repulsed,

as Alice felt, Susan spoke with mounting excitement. Alice felt distinctly uncomfortable. 'Can I speak to Caroline again?' she asked in a faint voice.

Her friend came to the phone. 'You've got Mum more animated than I've seen her in years,' she exclaimed. Her mother was speaking rapidly in the background. 'She'd love to get that book valued for you if you like.'

'There's a lot more to this story,' said Alice. 'I won't go into it now, but thanks for the info.' Putting down the phone, Alice jumped to find Hugo close behind her.

'Gosh!' he said. 'So this' – he picked up the book – 'is covered with human skin. Josephine Fernsby's at that. I never heard of such a thing. We need to see what else is written in here.' He made another attempt to ease apart the rest of the pages. 'What are they stuck together with? Seems to be some sort of grease. Look, the next few pages are free, although the grease has spoilt them, making the writing illegible.'

'Maybe because it's been near the radiator?' said Alice. 'That would melt the fat. Let's put it by the heat for a few minutes, see if we can unstick any more. I'm not touching it, though. You can.'

Hugo pulled a face. 'Given that it's so rare, we should take care not to damage it.' He carried the book to the radiator by the parlour window, dragging a coffee table over to rest the book on, open pages towards the heat. 'This will be interesting.'

In the kitchen, the couple made a coffee and sandwich each, both pretending they weren't dying to read what was in the book. After 10 minutes, they could wait no longer and returned to the parlour. Hugo picked it up. 'Some more pages are free, although quite a few are still clamped together. But I reckon we can get most apart if we're careful.'

He began to read. '"The notes of Dr Montmorency Eusebius Clement, surgeon, 1855. I thank the dedication of Mrs Clarimond Tucker, most excellent housekeeper, cook, chandler and assistant. Here I document the case of one Josephine Fernsby, whose body I was fortunate enough to procure. Her cause of death was mysterious, but I have solved the riddle. Josephine Fernsby gave her mortal remains to the cause of furthering medical research and also furthering my own dissection skills, and for that I am grateful. Opening her chest and abdominal cavity confirmed the presence of" – oh, I can't read this. He goes on, "The good beeswax candles are running out, but Mrs Tucker will make tallow ones.

'"She tells me we have a little mutton fat. The corpse has a goodly amount of hard fat around the kidneys and heart, which Mrs Tucker will render down and mix with the mutton grease to make more candles so I can continue my work." The next page I can't read. Then it says, "Thanks to her expert chandler skills, Mrs Tucker has produced 30 candles from the corpse fat. The stench is foul and they burn fast, but it is much preferable to the dark."'

Hugo broke off. 'A chandler is a candle-maker. Oh my God. Do you think those candles we used are made from Josephine's fat?'

'I genuinely want to vomit,' said Alice. 'We've been breathing in the scent of a human being's flesh.' She put her hand to her mouth. 'But go on.'

'Well, then there are diagrams, anatomical ones, pages and pages, and the writing is too small to read,' continued Hugo. Then he gasped. 'Here it is. Towards the end, it says, "As is my custom, this book shall be bound in Josephine Fernsby's skin. I have preserved a section from the dorsal area to give my bookbinder Mr Hulme in London. He will have it tanned and bind these pages into the book, which will go in my collection.'" Hugo waved the book. 'Could there be more than one of these?'

Alice had a thought. '"Dorsal" means back. The girl, when she appeared before us, had dark patches all over her front near her heart. And that wide, stained section across her shoulders. Blood! Where Dr Clement took her belly fat and the skin from her back. This is beyond barbaric.'

Although they no longer needed it, Alice built the fire back up and they sat side by side on the sofa discussing what to do next. On the mantlepiece, the clock showed it was nearly 4pm as the fire glowed in the grate, afternoon shadows gathering in the corners of the room. Rain fell steadily outside, dripping from the windowsills like a tap. Then movement by the curtain drew Alice's eyes and a figure stepped out of the gloom, once again in a blood-stained shroud. Today the girl's eyes were milky white marbles in sunken sockets, her feet bare and dirty. She held out her hands. 'Bury me,' she said clearly. 'Please, bury me.'

Alice clutched at Hugo's forearm as he swivelled to look. 'You see her?' she whispered. 'I do,' he nodded, his eyes on the girl.

'You hear her? Earlier when I thought she said "Buree" – she was saying "Bury me."'

The figure flickered and was gone.

'I suppose us burning the candles somehow released her ghost,' said Alice. 'Anyhow, our task is clear. We take the book and what's left of the candles, and we bury them in her grave.'

A shadow crossed Hugo's face. 'I don't think we can do that.'

Alice was taken aback. 'Why on earth not?'

'Because Dad had hoped this book would be here in the house and asked me to look for it. He tried to find it and failed, so gave us two weeks to locate it. He has a buyer with very deep pockets who wants to purchase this book...'

'So you knew all along the book was here?' said Alice, aghast.

'I didn't know what was so special about it – the

human skin. I thought the hand-written notes of a pioneering surgeon were what the collector wanted. No one was even certain the book existed at all.'

'Don't lean on the glass like that, sweetheart. The window frame is rotten...' Hugo's words on their first morning came back to Alice. 'That first day, you woke me with a cup of tea and said you hadn't seen the house. But you'd already had a good look round, hadn't you? Because you knew the upstairs window was dangerous.'

Hugo gave her a sidelong glance, like a naughty schoolboy who'd been caught out.

'And given that the book's so valuable, how come you were happy to warm it up so we could unstick the pages?' she continued. 'And why wouldn't you tell me we were looking for it?'

'Once a scientist, always a scientist. My curiosity got the better of me.' He shrugged. 'None of us are straightforward, are we? Dad said to keep it secret and I didn't question him. I can see why now. A book bound in the hide of a human being is beyond ghoulish.

'We can bury the candles. But I'm keeping the book

for Dad. He's flying back – he'll be here tomorrow.

'Ah – that's who you were on the phone to yesterday,' said Alice. 'No. We must do what's right. We're burying that book.' Taking a deep breath to overcome her revulsion, she picked it up. As she turned to leave the room, Hugo rose quickly, sore foot forgotten, and gripped her shoulder roughly with one hand. His mouth set in a tight line, he tried to prise the book from her fingers but she held it fast.

'We're disposing of this book properly,' said Alice, twisting free from his grip. 'You told me your dad bullied you, put you down for leaving medical school, laughed at you for wanting to go into journalism. He won't change. This won't make him respect you.'

'Spare me the cod psychoanalysis,' Hugo snarled. 'I promised Dad I'd get the book and I won't let him down.'

With a quick movement, Alice bolted to the fireplace and threw the volume into the grate, grabbing the poker and prodding it deep into the embers. The oily paper revived the fire, which flared orange, flames licking around the book, the fat helping it to burn. As fire bit into the leather Hugo snatched the poker from her and tried desperately to dig the book out. Now a small fireball, it glowed brightly, then sunk into the grate, a mass of charred remains.

Hugo's eyes flashed. 'You bitch! Take it. Take the remnants and do what you like with them. I don't care.' Defeated, he dropped into a chair.

Alice ran from the room to pack, throwing her things in her rucksack anyhow. Downstairs she took the cashbox, into which she put the remaining candle before scooping up the book's ashes and fragments of leather from the hearth with a ladle, ignoring Hugo sulking like a child in the wing chair.

She wasn't going to say goodbye, taking a palette knife with a shabby wooden handle from the cutlery drawer as she went through the kitchen on her way out.

Mercifully, the rain had stopped although thunderclouds rolled across the sky, bruised and ready to open. Alice's heart speeded up as she neared the cemetery. The gate stood ajar and the place was silent save for the lilting song of a lone robin in the yew tree she passed under and the rustling of her feet in the stiff grass. Alice was grateful there was still enough light to find the grave and that she didn't have to venture too far into the home of the dead. 'Sorry, Josephine,' she said as she reached the headstone. 'The ground will be too hard to dig very deep, but I'll do my best.'

Kneeling on a plastic bag and using the palette knife to scrape at the frosty soil, Alice managed to make a hole half an inch deep. Then, somehow, the ground grew soft and Alice found she was able to dig a gap large enough to fit the cashbox. Giving the candle and bits of charred leather and paper one last look, she tucked the box into the hole. 'Rest in peace, Josephine,' she said, scraping the soil over. There came a faint sigh and, as she rose, there in front of her was the girl, sallow of cheek but whole and smiling, in a full-skirted dress of periwinkle blue. As Alice watched, the figure shimmered and was gone.

Alice shouldered her backpack and set off to walk to the train station. Though she had no idea when the next train was due, she'd happily wait any length of time to get away from Hugo, his family and Emebury.

To get back to her life in London which, along with being single, no longer seemed so bad after all. And her early escape meant she didn't have to face Hugo's father, nor tell Hugo about her last meeting with him, when she'd bumped into Dr Gastrell at the British Museum. He'd caught her arm and purred a greeting into her ear, and she'd put his palm cupping her breast down as an accident, the result of him moving out of the way to allow someone past.

Not anymore.

Two

ME Two

'IF YOU MET YOUR double, James, what would you do?'

Henry, a friend since our time at a London university, leaned forward expectantly. I regarded my companion with interest. His pale complexion was even more bloodless than usual, the high forehead with fair hair swept back emphasising the air of intelligence I remembered from our student days. He raised his light eyebrows quizzically. 'Well?'

'Given that we're used to seeing a mirror image of ourselves in the, er, mirror, I suspect I may not recognise myself straight away,' I replied with a half-smile.

Henry stretched his lips tight in a grimace. 'I'm serious. If you met yourself – not someone who looked like you, but who *was* you, what would you

79

do?'

I was fond of Henry. We'd been close as psychology students a decade ago, although our lives had diverged since then. I'd qualified as a child psychologist and moved to the Surrey countryside, while Henry had taken a job as a data analyst in the City. Being an anxious person and a great worrier due, I believed, to his difficult start in life, Henry had struggled with his exams but done well in his finals with the help of a little medication. I'd been surprised to hear he'd taken work in such a high-pressure environment, but people can surprise you and he was earning very well – much better than me.

But my old friend had been through a trauma recently and had texted with a request to drive down to my place for the afternoon for what he called 'a dose of my no-nonsense chat', along with a calming stroll in the fields.

We'd taken a walk in the thin March sun, following it with a ploughman's lunch at the local pub. For his visits on chilly days, Henry normally enjoyed a fire in the living room, but today, as I'd knelt to assemble the logs and firelighters, he'd said, scrunching his brows into a frown, 'Actually, I rather you didn't, if you don't mind.' I understood his opposition to the fire this particular day. Then, taking one of the pair of armchairs by the hearth, he'd sighed and sat back.

Seeing he was ready to talk, I'd made us each a coffee and taken my seat opposite.

That's when the question about doubles came up.

'Henry, is your enquiry related to what happened in London?'

He nodded, seeming to fold in on himself inside his sage designer jumper. Then he widened his blue eyes. 'Look, I'll just tell you the story. Then I'd like to hear your take on it.'

This is what he told me.

'You know I bought a flat in Kensington – you came over once, when I lived there with Janine. Fair tore me in two when she dumped me, but still. It's the top floor of a house off the King's Road, two bedrooms, huge kitchen. A conversion.

'You and I haven't seen each other for a couple of years, James, and about six months ago, at my sister

Sadie's son's fifth birthday party, I stupidly leaped on to the bouncy castle with him. Jumping up and down, little Josh and I smashed heads and there was so much blood I thought I'd killed him! Turns out the blood was coming from me, and Sadie took me to A&E to get stitched up. Got a long scar here, on my temple.

'That was a Friday. I felt woozy for a couple of days – mild concussion, the doctor said. I slept a lot but felt OK by the Sunday. That's when things began to get weird.

'I had an urge for a good, hot shower – my first since the accident – so into the bathroom I went. Head back with my eyes shut, relishing the water flowing over my face and shoulders, I soaped my chest and arms, then reached for the shampoo. Rubbing both hands in my hair, suddenly I was aware that my chest was being soaped again, with firm strokes from strong fingers. My eyes sprang open – there were two hands rubbing me down. Even through the running water and soap bubbles, I could see they were my own hands. Dropping my actual hands from my hair in shock, I instinctively went to grab the fingers moving on my chest – but they simply weren't there anymore.

'Too shocked to cry out or even turn off the shower, I stumbled out naked, then ran out of the bathroom into the hall. There had to be someone there! Wildly, I rushed into each of the bedrooms, looking under the beds and inside wardrobes. Nothing. The lounge and kitchen were equally empty.

'Being a bit paranoid, as you know, I always lock my main door with the key when I'm at home and shoot the bolt at the top. Panting now, I could see the bolt was fully drawn and, trying the door, that was still locked.

'Shivering, I grabbed my robe from the bedroom door and collapsed on the bed to think. I stretched out my hands in front of me. There's that saying, "I know X like the back of my hand", yet most people probably haven't spent much time gazing at theirs. I have. You know I play piano? My music teacher used to say I had "pianist hands" – long, nimble fingers and a wide span, even as a youngster. Hours, days, years toiling at the keyboard. So I do know my own hands thoroughly – and I couldn't fool myself.

'There had been no intruder.

'My own hands had been in two places at once – in

my hair and on my chest.

'Except that was impossible. What had I noticed beyond the hands? I tried to remember. It had been hard to see, what with the strong, spread-out flow of water from my waterfall shower and all the suds. The hands seemed to be attached to wrists and forearms, as they would be if I was actually washing myself... No. I shook my head. This was madness! I was simply disorientated after my accident.

'Laughing at my foolishness, I dressed and went to the supermarket.

'About three months later, I had a date in town in the afternoon and was walking towards my car, which was parked a street away. Being a bank holiday, the roads were quiet and, unusually, my white Audi was the only vehicle on that stretch of road. Ahead of me by 20 yards strode a male figure. Tall with a lilting walk, he had short fair hair, wore a smart camel coat and was swinging a set of car keys – I could hear them jingling in his hand. "That coat looks good on him," I thought. "Very like mine at home." To my surprise, the man stopped in front of my car and, as he dug the key into the lock and I saw him in profile, I realised I was looking at myself!

'"Hey!"' I called, sprinting towards the figure as it opened the car door, climbed in and slammed the door shut with a bang.

'Drawing level with the car, my heart thudding in my chest, I placed my hand on the driver's seat window and bent to look in.

'It was, of course, empty. I had a strong physical reaction to this and felt like throwing up.

'I don't know what that was about, but I couldn't bring myself to get into the car, so I caught the bus instead.

'By now I was starting to seriously question my sanity. The event put me right off my Audi. I got rid of it and bought a red MG – I came over in it today. It's parked outside your front garden.

'Then came the business you know about, which happened a fortnight ago.

'It had been a tough week at work and I wanted a quiet Friday night home alone in front of the TV with a couple of beers and a takeaway curry. I hadn't seen "me" in any form for a while and had put the episodes down to the after-effects of my head-knock.

'It must have been 1am when I climbed into bed, left my phone charging on the floor and switched off my bedside lamp. The bed was warm and cosy and I drifted off to sleep.

'Then suddenly I was awake, feeling as shocked as I would if someone had thrown a bucket of ice water in my face. I was in bed, but something was badly wrong. I lay on my back, head sunk into the pillow, hands clutching the quilt at my throat. Thanks to my blackout blinds, the darkness of the room, so comforting hours earlier, now served as cover for something I could sense absolutely should not be there but was, nevertheless. A chill seeped into my exposed cheeks, nose and forehead and I shuddered beneath the bedding.

'I strained my ears. Silence. Should I get up? *Could* I get up?

'After a minute or two, nothing had happened but, rather than switch on the bedside lamp, I stretched a hand down to my phone on the floor. It was just out of reach. Leaning the upper half of my body out of bed, I went to grab it with my right hand and the phone sprang to life, the large numbers of the clock showing 3:34. The light from the screen illuminated the area immediately around it – and I saw there was something in the dark shadows under the bed.

'Long – as long as the bed, almost. Bulky.

'A figure.

'I screamed, the shrill sound from my throat frightening me, and dropped the phone, which landed with a plop on the carpet. Within seconds, the display died and the room was in darkness once again.

'I didn't dare reach for the phone. Instead, I fell back against the pillow, my eyes staring into the blackness, every muscle as taut as piano wire, my teeth clenched together in fear.

'From directly beneath me came a series of soft sounds. The space is shallow under a bed, necessitating the coordination of feet, shoulders and buttocks to slide a body out if one was under there – one, two three; one, two, three; one, two, three. The sounds came closer and closer to the edge of the bed – the right side, where I lay. Frozen to the spot with terror, I understood that the figure had wriggled out and was now standing up. Steady breathing revealed it was bent over me.

'Somehow, my arm shot out and switched on the lamp. There, in the pool of light, stood – me. As the figure and I stared at each other, I saw this was a different version of me. Me Two wore a zipped-up grey hoodie with a rip in the shoulder, its fair hair in the shaved-up-the-back-and-sides skunk style I associated with builders. A butterfly tattoo spread across its throat, like a parody of a bow tie.

'Although Me Two's face was expressionless, it grasped my quilt, yanked it off, then took my arm and hauled me to my feet. Too shocked and surprised to do anything other than follow its directions, when it picked up my clothes from a chair, flung them at me and pushed me urgently towards the bedroom door, I took the garments but don't remember how I got int the hall. Dressing quickly, I snatched up my car and door keys, although I didn't bother to lock my front door, and ran outside to the MG. Then I drove around the silent streets in a daze while whatever was about to happen came to pass.

'The rest you know, James. A fire started in my bedroom – the police couldn't work out how – and my bedroom door was jammed closed. They tell me

I'd have suffocated or been burnt alive if I'd been in there.

'I'm staying with Sadie, but I won't go back to my flat, even when the fire damage has been rectified.

'I haven't seen Me Two since, thank God. But did he – I – save my life, or did he – I – start the fire anyway? All this goes round and round in my head. I can't sleep. I'm off work. And I haven't told this to anybody, although Sadie can see I'm in a right old state and doesn't know what to do with me.

'So I thought I'd come to you, Dr Smith, with your training in psychotherapeutic theory and treatment methods. And you're an old friend who's always been loyal and straight-talking. What do you think? About me? And about doubles?'

Henry had spoken without pause for over an hour and my concerns for his mental health were great by the time he'd reached the end of his tale. I'd been smiling and nodding at points to encourage Henry to relate the full account of his situation as he saw it, while also flicking through a mental index of which of my psychiatrist colleagues would be most suitable to give my friend the help he so clearly needed.

Looking up, I saw Henry had that expectant expression again. I began to sigh, then changed it into a cough.

'I'm not a medical man, as you know,' I began, 'but I do wonder if your bang on the head may have affected the part of your brain dealing with vision, leading to the' – I chose my words carefully so as not to cause offence – 'sensation of seeing your own doppelganger, or double. After all, these occurrences began after your accident, as you say.

'I'm not sure this is a matter for psychology,' I continued, 'but I am aware of a variety of people who believe they've seen their double. For example, Percy Shelley, the poet, reported spotting his.'

'Yes,' replied Henry, with a miserable sniff, 'I read about that. Shelley witnessed his double trying to strangle his wife, Mary, one night. And the man saw his doppelganger again a few days before he drowned at sea.' Henry dashed away a tear, of fear or anger or both. 'I've read that seeing your double is often a portent that you're about to die.'

This wasn't a mental route I wanted Henry to go down. 'Ah,' I said, 'that can't be true in your case. Your double – if indeed it did appear – saved your life.'

'Yes,' he said more brightly. 'Good point. What do you think about what it was wearing the third time, in my bedroom?'

'I suppose,' I mused, 'that could have been an Alternative Henry. You and Sadie were born in a poor part of Bradford and the death of your parents – sorry, I know this is awful for you, but you did tell me this – from a heroin overdose led to the two of you being adopted. If you'd stayed there, rather than ended up in a well-off family who could afford a house near good schools and the like, maybe that's who you'd have become and your mind conjured that image up. A kind of complicated embodiment of survivor guilt.'

'Survivor guilt?'

'Yes, it's not uncommon. You survived but your parents didn't, and surviving, especially thriving, while others perished can lead us to feel guilty. Perhaps the "you" in the camel coat was a halfway house between Current Henry and Alternative Henry.'

Night was falling outside. Henry turned towards

the window and I followed his gaze. 'Jilly will be home from work soon and she'd love you to stay for dinner,' I said. This wasn't actually true – my wife would want to throw off her shoes and flop in front of her favourite soap with a glass of wine and not speak to anyone for an hour, but I didn't want Henry to feel any more alone than he already did.

Reading my expression, Henry got to his feet. 'No thanks. I'd rather make a start on the drive back to London,' he said, looking around for his jacket. Walking him to the door, I explained that I'd email the names of a couple of professionals he could speak to, including a neurologist acquaintance.

On the doorstep, my friend shook my hand warmly. 'It means a lot to me that you listened to my tale, James,' he said. 'Even though I bet you secretly think I'm nuts!'

Henry certainly seemed lighter than when he'd arrived, I thought, closing the door.

Returning to the lounge, I watched out of the window as Henry climbed into his sports car, gave me one last wave over his shoulder and drove off down the lane.

Smiling to myself, I turned to go into the kitchen. Then I stopped short and gasped.

There, in the chair he'd just vacated, sat Henry, grinning and tugging at the zip of his grey hoodie, the tattooed butterfly's body bulging on his Adam's apple.

THREE

THE MAN ON THE CLAPHAM OMNIBUS

'I HAVEN'T SEEN YOU on this bus before. Are you new to the area?'

Jake shuffled his feet uneasily and angled his lean knees away from the man sitting to his left. Oblivious to Jake's discomfort, the man spread his heavy thighs comfortably, nudging the youth's legs over even further.

Getting the bus home late from his Thursday shift at the coffee shop meant Jake met his fair share of so-called nutters on the bus. While not exactly a nutter, this man, with his fleshy face, thick neck bulging from the collar of a dingy white shirt, crumpled grey suit fraying at the cuffs and the smell of sweat with an undertone of stale booze had not been welcome when he'd plopped into the seat next to Jake. Especially as Jake knew there were empty seats behind where the man could have taken up as much room as he liked without disturbing any other poor sod.

The bus meandered through Clapham's dimly lit streets. With its grassy common and new bars popping up daily, the area was somewhere Jake would love to live if he ever got the kind of job that stretched to the hefty rent required. As it was, he was going home to his downmarket bit of south London several miles away, where so much chewing gum stuck to the pavements you brought a gob indoors with you on your shoe after every journey.

Jake felt a dig in his side. The man was gazing at him, wanting an answer to his question. 'I, er, no – I often get this bus home from work.' Don't engage with a nutter on the bus – that's the unwritten rule. Give them as little attention as you can get away with and they'll lose interest. But Jake had already given away too much and cursed to himself as the man continued.

'Work? Doing what? You look like an accountant. Can't be much accounting to be done at 11 o'clock at night.' The man shook with mirth at his own wit.

People often mistook Jake, with his tidy, smooth hair and tidy, smooth complexion, for a trainee teacher. So this was a change. In fact, he'd failed his law degree at university and got the job at the cafe to buy himself some time while he thought about what else to do with his life.

Despite himself, Jake said, 'Actually, I work at a coffee shop close to town.' Damn! He'd done it again.

'Not in Clapham, then? That's where I always get on the bus. In fact, I *am* the Man on the Clapham Omnibus.' He chuckled. 'Don't worry, son. A joke. You're what, 17? Way too young to know what that is.'

Jake felt exasperated. Why did people think he was a kid? 'I'm 24, actually, and I do know that term,' he said indignantly. 'It was coined in the 1930s to mean "the view of the reasonable man in the street."'

Only three more stops and then I can escape, thought Jake. The guy is probably lonely, so don't be rude – be kind, Mum always used to say. Be kind to those less fortunate than you. Although Mum was long gone; dad too. Their death in a car crash before Jake's finals had delivered a nerve-shattering shock and he'd done so poorly in the exams the university couldn't even bump his marks up to a third-class degree on compassionate grounds.

Pressure on Jake's thigh told him the man was pressing his against it firmly. He looked into the ruddy face but the expression hadn't changed from benign interest. This wasn't a sexual overture; simply a guy who had no sense of personal space.

The man spoke again, peering closely at Jake, who drew back in alarm. 'Actually, I've seen you before,' he said slowly, tapping his temple with a forefinger. 'Give me a sec – it'll come to me.'

Another bus stop. A woman clutching a fat, panting Corgi swept on and sat behind Jake and the man. Jake felt such relief when the name of his stop flashed up on the digital display in front of them. He rose without a word, expecting the man to swing his legs to one side so Jake could pass, the usual bus etiquette. Instead, the man lifted his broad face with its stubbled grey chin towards Jake and grimaced, displaying a gap in his yellow teeth at the side. 'Yes. Something to do with – with...'

'Excuse me,' said Jake. Actually, he wanted to yell, 'Shift your bloody legs out of the way, you twat!' But he was going to be kind, in remembrance of Mum.

The man's jaw continued to work, the cogs in his memory turning slowly as he kept his eyes on Jake. He still didn't move so Jake pushed roughly past, stamping on the man's foot accidentally on purpose. 'You shouldn't do that, son,' barked the man. 'I reckon you and me have some unfinished business. If I could just remember what exactly...' Pain exploded at the bottom of Jake's spine. The man had thumped him hard.

Jake darted to the bus doorway and gripped the pole next to it, knuckles white with rage. The bus doors hissed open and Jake stepped onto the pavement, his breath coming in gasps.

He was furious. Yet again, he hadn't spoken his mind. Yet again, he'd let himself down. Yet again, he'd failed. Story of my life, he thought as he hurried down the darkened roads to his flat.

His two flatmates were in bed and Jake felt shaken after his encounter with the man on the bus. Of course he didn't recognise Jake, unless he'd been to the coffee shop. What could he do to feel better? Making himself a cheese sandwich, he set it by his laptop on his desk. Switching on the machine, he began to pull up photos of Sally, his last girlfriend. Guilt, guilt, guilt. He'd treated her so badly when all she'd done was love him. He thought back to their last conversation a few months ago.

'It's been a year and you still won't let me see your place,' Sally had said. 'What do you think I'm going to do – move my stuff in while you're on the loo?'

Jake had lowered his eyes. 'I have to take things slowly. Getting close is hard for me.'

'And keeping this distant is hard for *me*. I get that you're scared of being hurt since you lost your parents. But I have no plans to leave. You can trust me.'

'That's exactly what someone who couldn't be trusted would say,' he'd muttered. It had descended into a row and they'd lain back-to-back that night at Sally's.

Lying awake, Jake made a decision.

'The truth is,' he said next morning while Sally pulled on her jeans, 'I've met someone else. One of my managers at work – we've been seeing each other for a while. Sorry.' He found his jacket and made for the door.

'Sorry? Is that it, after a year? How could you be so

callous? Leading me on? Lying? Just go!' She flopped down on the bed on her back and began to weep silently, tears running down the sides of her face onto the pillow. 'You're not who I thought you were.'

Hiding his own misery, Jake let himself out. Yes, he was a liar. He wasn't seeing his boss or anyone else. But he couldn't take any more pressure from Sally. He needed to sort his emotions out before he could become seriously involved with someone. That hadn't been kind of him at all, but he was too mixed up to be all sensitive new man about it. She'd get over him, anyway, soon enough.

A fortnight later, Angie, his uni mate who'd introduced him to Sally, called him. 'What have you done?' she yelled down the phone 'You've broken that girl. She can't stop crying and won't get out of bed. Won't go into work and I can't get her to eat. Why didn't you at least end it with Sally before you started shagging around? You know she's vulnerable, having lost her mum. You're just a–'

Jake didn't reply, stabbing the line dead and blocking Angie's number. He didn't need this, an attack from his friend. She'd been his only pal in

London. Without her, and especially without Sally, he felt very lonely indeed.

The last he'd heard from Angie was an email two months on. 'I hope you're proud of yourself,' she'd written. 'Sally has had a total mental breakdown and is in a psychiatric hospital. She won't speak to anyone – not even her dad.' Jake hadn't read any further and had deleted the email.

One of the things that had drawn him and Sally together was that they'd both lost close family, although to Jake, she was very fortunate to still have her dad. Her old man had problems, had been struggling with life since his wife's death and taken to drink. But he doted on his only daughter and was always FaceTiming to see how his precious Sal-sal was, although Jake would always duck away from the screen when her dad called and had just about managed not to be introduced to him. But what could Jake do? To him it seemed better for both of them if they parted.

Jake had planned to look at some of the photos from when he and Sally were happy. Fool, he thought. You think that will help? Shoulders drooping, he clicked the folder shut and began an online job search instead. Going over old relationship ground would most likely drag him even further down, reminding him what he'd thrown away.

A month passed in a flurry of work shifts and rows with his flatmates over stolen food and Jake forgot all about the man.

The autumn rain was falling heavily and Jake was grateful to leave it behind and hop onto the warm bus after another late shift. The bottom deck was empty, so he headed for his favourite seat, second from the front behind the space for prams and wheelchairs, thankful the late hour meant the area was free from screaming children.

Ahead was the screen that showed every area of the bus in turn, changing views every few seconds like an eye blinking. As Jake watched, there was the front of the top deck, where a teal-haired woman stared hard at her phone. Blink. Two teenage boys play-fought on the upstairs back seat. Blink. There was Jake on the screen. After eight hours serving entitled, belligerent customers, he looked wan and tired, his face as ashen as his light hair.

Sighing, he dug out the free newspaper one of the bus's occupants had stuffed down the side of the seat. He'd spread it wide to read when suddenly, there was the tatty man from a few weeks ago, lurching through the doors after a guy in a hoodie and making his way towards Jake.

The man plonked himself down. He wore the same crumpled grey suit, his chin still bristling with stubble, and again he reeked of sweat and stale booze. 'I was hoping I'd run into you,' he murmured, as though he and Jake had known each other for years and he hadn't punched Jake that Thursday. With a tight smile, Jake shifted further against the bus wall, hoping to give the man enough room to keep them from touching. Instead, the man took all the space offered and pressed himself once again to Jake's side, arm to arm, thigh to thigh. 'Like I said before, we have unfinished business.'

As he spoke, Jake noticed with alarm that the thigh pressed to his was cold, as cold as meat on a butcher's slab fresh from the fridge. He could feel the chill even through his overcoat. The same went for the plump arm squashed against his. He looked closer at the man.

Rather than the red apple cheeks of before, the face was pallid and puffy. And as if the whiff of body odour and booze wasn't offensive enough, beneath it was something else, another smell that made Jake's nose wrinkle with disgust, but he couldn't put his finger on it.

'We have someone in common, you and I,' the man was saying. No we don't, thought Jake. You're pissed and I'm knackered. He tuned the man's words out and turned to look through the window at the wet streets, the raindrops running down the glass making it more difficult to get his bearings. It was so dark tonight. Ah, was that the post office? Just five more stops, then.

The man was speaking and as Jake turned back from the window, his eyes alighted on the TV screen in front of him, with its rolling display of Scenes From The Bus.

Blink.

Downstairs at the back, Hoodie Guy munched on a burger, the meat-and-pickle smell sharp on the air.

Blink.

The bus driver, glancing at his wing mirror and

running one hand over his bald scalp before returning it to the steering wheel.

Blink.

Jake in his navy coat, pale and jaded as always. The seat next to him was empty, the blue patterned back clearly visible by his shoulder.

What?

Blink.

The camera had moved to the top deck, but Jake felt his pulse quicken, his heart fluttering in his chest like a bird trapped in a hedge. Beside him, the frosty pressure from the man's body seemed to seep into Jake's bones, chilling him to the marrow. The man talked on, but Jake couldn't focus on his words.

The bus slithered to a halt. The teenagers clattered down the stairs and leapt off, the blue-haired woman close behind them. Hoodie Guy passed them and left the bus. Now it was just him and the man travelling in the vehicle.

Jake's brain raced as he tried to make sense of his predicament. There was, apparently, no one next to him on the seat, yet Jake could see the man, feel his voice reverberating through his bulky frame and vibrating against Jake's upper arm. Squinting to look at the passing shops, Jake noted he had just two stops to go. He'd get off early and walk the rest of the way. Feeling marginally better now he had a plan, Jake tensed his feet and knees and began to rise from his seat. At that moment, the bus gave a lurch, throwing him off balance and back into his seat as it came to an abrupt stop.

Then the lights snapped out, plunging the bus into darkness.

Up until that point, Jake hadn't been aware of the sound of the bus's engine, the throb and whoosh as it travelled along the roads and the idling sound as it waited for passengers to alight and depart. But as the engine cut out, silence fell over the bus like a shroud. The driver will make an announcement any second, Jake thought wildly. Not only did none come, but the front of the bus was so quiet it was as though the driver had dematerialised.

Jake made to tense his legs again, planning to jump up and escape the bus any way he could. But the connection between his brain and leg muscles could have been severed for all the effect that had.

He couldn't move his arms either, his hands stiff and immobile in his lap on top of the crumpled newspaper.

They must have stopped in a street – Jake knew the bus route – yet where were the streetlights? The houses, with their lighted front windows? The cars, headlamps brightening the road? The blackness was so total they could have been buried underground.

To his left, a cloud of frosty air enveloped his ear and he realised the man had bent his lips close. 'This is nice,' he whispered. 'Intimate. We can have a proper chat now. About our shared... *situation*.'

To Jake's horror, a damp, cold hand enclosed one of his and squeezed it and, as it did so, a stench of wet earth and rotten flesh rose to meet his nostrils.

The man's base note he hadn't been able to identify earlier.

'You know someone who's special to me,' breathed the man. 'Who was special to *you*. And you're going to pay for what you've done.' Icy hands fumbled for Jake's thin neck, encircled it and began to squeeze.

A scream stuck in Jake's throat as the hands tightened and he shut his eyes, clawing at the fat fingers in an attempt to peel them off, rocking and twisting in his seat as he tried to get to his feet.

Then the hands were gone and he found himself standing in the aisle, blinking in the harsh strip lighting of the bus.

Jake lurched towards the doorway, his legs barely holding him upright.

'Hey, fella,' called the bus driver. 'Are you drunk? Get a hold of the handrail. I'm not opening the doors until you're steady on your feet. I don't want any accidents.'

'I'm good,' spluttered Jake. 'Please just open the doors.' He planted his feet firmly, stabilising himself with both hands on the door poles on either side and trying to look like the sober, respectable person he knew himself to be. He didn't dare glance back at his seat.

'Only,' grunted the driver, 'four weeks ago on a Thursday about this time, there was an accident a few stops up the road – a bad accident. A man stepped off my bus right into the path of a cyclist and was killed outright. It was bloody awful, I can tell you. I had to take time off work. Just came back today.'

The driver opened his own door a crack, stuck his head out and peered at Jake, pushing his glasses up the bridge of his broad nose with a forefinger. 'Weren't you the guy sitting next to the bloke on the CCTV? You were chatting to him. Wasn't a mate of yours, was he? Old guy in a grey suit?'

'I don't remember,' stammered Jake. 'Let me out, please!'

The doors rattled apart and he almost fell down the bus step to the pavement. Behind him, the doors closed with a clatter. Through the window, Jake eyeballed the seat he'd vacated.

It was empty.

Rucksack bouncing on his back, Jake didn't stop running until he reached his front door. Empty pizza boxes in the kitchen and two wide open bedroom doors told him his flatmates, both nurses, had nipped home for food and gone on their night shifts. That at least meant Jake could lock the front door, which he did, sliding the bolts home at the top and bottom, although he wasn't sure why he felt compelled to do so.

He was home and safe, but he didn't feel good.

Something nibbled at the edge of his mind and he had to tackle it. With a sinking feeling in the pit of his stomach, Jake flew into his room and fired up his laptop. He and Sally had exchanged family pictures one night and he'd saved hers. Clicking around the screen frantically, he tried folder after folder, vowing to label his photos properly.

Ah, here it was. Sally as a girl leading her pony, with glossy auburn pigtails and that wide smile she'd grown into, the large teeth now perfectly in proportion to her heart-shaped face. Sally as a teenager with her mum and dad, three smart, slender people leaning on a silver BMW and looking like they had the world at their feet.

And here was Sally at her graduation a couple of years ago, nestling against a man with an arm around her shoulders. Jake clicked to enlarge the snap and his stomach shook.

It was the same man from the earlier family photo. But instead of looking slim and healthy, he looked 20 years older than in the first picture, even though it was only a decade on. The ruddy-cheeked face, stubbled chin, sausage fingers and crumpled grey suit were sadly familiar.

When Jake heard heavy steps tramp slowly up the stairs minutes later, he knew who it was.

FOUR

HEADS YOU LOSE

PRESSING A TISSUE TO my streaming eyes, I drew my knees up under my chin and gave a howl of such lingering pain that my sister Abbie ran in and crouched down beside where I lay on the sofa.

'Oh, Lucy,' she said softly, the concern in her amber eyes going some way to ease my wounded heart. Tucking the fleecy blanket that covered me around my haunches, Abbie leaned over to hug me, resting her cheek on my hair. 'I understand that you miss him, and that it hurts like hell. I felt the same when Dermot left.'

That angered and upset me, prompting a fresh stream of tears. 'You can't possibly know how I feel,' I gulped, blowing my nose noisily. 'Dermot was only gone for a fortnight, then he reappeared with an engagement ring. Logan ran off nearly two months ago and I've no idea where to. Not a squeak from him. Dermot had been at his mum's round the corner, grappling with his commitmentphobia. *So* not the same.'

I shut my eyes and turned away from Abbie to bury my cheek in the back sofa cushion, partly to avoid the smug expression which I knew she wouldn't be able to stop creeping into her features. Four years older than me, I loved my sister but, as with most siblings, competition was never far from the surface with us. Yet she did genuinely care for me, helping with my biology homework, lending me her favourite skinny jeans and sorting out the bullies at school when Mum had been too busy.

Abbie sat back and I heard her settle on the floor, probably in the lotus position she favoured now she was a yoga instructor. 'Well, let's see if Dermot can make it to the altar,' she said impatiently, looping a dark curl behind her ear. 'The jury's still out on whether he'll get there.

'Anyway,' she continued, giving me a hearty slap on the bum. 'I've got a present for you. Or rather Rowena, my new yoga client, gave me a box with some fun stuff in she thought you might like.'

I remembered Rowena. I'd met her briefly in Reception last week when I went to pick Abbie up from her premises. She and my sister were becoming friends and I'd noticed Rowena's slate-coloured eyes widen imperceptibly under her thick black fringe as I nodded hello to her at Abbie's introduction.

'Ow, you cow!' Laughing in spite of myself, I turned towards my sister and sat up.

'Yay!' she said. 'Is that a ghost of a smile I see? Remember to do your affirmations. They do work and they'll help boost your mood. Repeat after me: "I am a being of love and light. I radiate love and I attract love in turn. I am serene and content and good things are drawn to me."'

Mechanically, I echoed her words out loud as I trudged upstairs to get dressed. Abbie believed that, at 19, I shouldn't be so fixated on one guy, especially one that had promised me the sun, moon and stars but then vanished off the face of the Earth. We'd only been together a few weeks, but now I understood what the love songs said about how being in someone's arms felt like home.

And home had become an odd concept to me. Dad had died when Abbie and I were girls, and Mum had spent so much time at work in order to feed and clothe us that you could say Abbie was my little mother substitute. We still lived in the three-bed semi we'd grown up in, but just after my 18th birthday, my last exams over, Mum had informed us that her child-rearing days were finished and she was off to Benidorm to open a bar with her new boyfriend, Javier. That had been four months ago.

Restless and unsure what to do with myself after her departure and feeling less and less keen to leave home and take up my uni place at the other end of the country in the autumn, Logan had been exactly the distraction from real life and grown-up decisions I'd needed. Mum would not have approved of his blond dreadlocks, shocking pink clown trousers and black nail varnish.

'But you're not here, Mum, are you, so you can just bugger off,' I said to the air as I pulled on my clothes, squashing down the jolt of pain I recognised as intermingled Mum loss and Logan loss with an undercurrent of Dad misery. Anyway, it was Saturday morning and I was hungry.

In the kitchen, I sat at the marble-topped island in the middle of the room digging into my porridge as Abbie came in with a large cardboard box. 'I told Rowena you were feeling low after being dumped,' she said, plonking it on the table, 'and she mentioned that she was decluttering and thought you might like these. We can take anything you don't want to the charity shop.'

I wasn't sure I liked Rowena after the strange, cold way she'd regarded me, but there's something about a box filled with items you didn't put there yourself which is always intriguing.

Catching my scowl, Abbie put a hand on my arm. 'Rowena's proving to be a great new friend and it's important to me that you get on. We've had coffee a few times and she's a good listener. She's one of the few people who lets me talk about Dad without turning away. I think you'll like her.'

If my sister was that keen on this woman, I'd put my reservations aside for now. 'If you say so.'

Pushing my empty bowl away, I folded back the box's four flaps and took out the items one by one.

A couple of spiral-bound notebooks, navy blue and speckled with tiny, embossed silver stars. 'Lovely!' I declared, flicking through each before laying them on the side. 'Rowena makes those,' beamed Abbie, busying herself with the kettle. 'And the jewellery. She has a stall in the market on a Saturday. She thought those would be perfect for your colouring.'

I lifted out a black cord necklace with its round wooden pendant along with a matching bracelet. 'I love the tree drawn – or is it burnt? – on the front of these,' I exclaimed. 'That's generous of her.' Trying the bracelet on, I felt mean about the misgivings I'd had about Rowena. She seemed a kind, thoughtful soul.

At the back were two boxes. I picked up the smaller one and peered inside. It contained a pot, made of cast iron with three pointed legs and a top with triangular holes in. 'What's this?' I tipped it out and the lid fell off to reveal a bowl.

'Mmm – maybe an incense burner?' replied Abbie, looking up from making tea. 'Fancy a cuppa?'

Setting the pot down, I reached for the last box, which was on its side. It was black, rectangular, maybe a foot tall and weighed several pounds. 'Heavy! What's in here – someone's head?' I joked, shaking the box as I lifted it clear. Loose inside, the single object slipped from side to side, then its weight broke through the thin cardboard base. I caught it in my palm and slid it out.

'Wow,' I exclaimed, setting the item down by the incense burner. It was indeed a head – a full-sized, masculine one in green glass, hollow with a thick rim around the neck area. Wide-set, blank, almond eyes with moulded rims, a perky nose and full, parted lips. 'This must be worth a few quid. Surely it's vintage? Why would Rowena give me this? And what am I supposed to do with it?'

Handing me my tea, Abbie put her elbows on the table in front of the head and leaned her chin on her knuckles. 'He's quite beautiful,' she sighed, smoothing a hand across the curve of the bald head and around the back. 'And look! He has ears.' She tapped one. 'I guess these were used to display hats in shops in olden times. It'll make a cool place to store your around-ear headphones. Cooler than one of those polystyrene heads.'

Staring into the empty spaces that served as eyes, a shiver ran down my spine. 'I'll put it on the bookcase for now,' I said, lifting the thing gingerly and transporting it to the top of the low wooden shelves at the back of the room. 'There! Who's a pretty boy then?' The glass face regarded me blankly and I turned away to take a better look at the other items from the box.

Abbie and I gave the house a cursory clean – it was my turn to vacuum, unfortunately – then we did our usual Saturday food shop before TV, dinner and bed. Life should surely be more exciting at our age, but I was still mourning the loss of Logan and ignored my friends' urging to get 'back out there', preferring to hunker down at home with my big sister. Her fiancé Dermot was in Devon for work this week so she was happy to stay home with me tonight.

Wriggling into a comfortable position in bed, I forced myself to think objectively about Logan, hoping I could reach some kind of resolution in my mind. I wanted to go over our weeks together.

That smiley, cheeky profile photo delivered a punch to my gut the second I saw it on the dating app.

At our first meeting, the shiny-haired blond of the snap seemed to sport a slightly different saucy grin to the boy in front of me and the dreads hairdo was unexpected.

An hour in, I found out why. 'That was a random model photo I found online,' admitted Logan, chuckling. 'Thought I'd use it as my profile pic and see what happened. And it brought me you, gorgeous girl,' he continued, placing a finger on my lips to shush me when I opened them to protest.

After all, it was embarrassing that I'd immediately messaged someone who was so handsome he looked like a model – and that was because he *was* one. Shallow Lucy! Anyway, I told myself, Logan did look quite like the photo, although his nose was a little wider at the tip, the teeth more gappy.

I ignored what that dishonesty might say about him as a person. And I ignored what ignoring it might say about me.

Logan lived in a flat on his own in the next town and we'd meet up, cycle to his place and spend days at a time there lost in each other. He said the 'L' word first and we talked about visiting Peru in the autumn, trekking up Machu Picchu together.

Abbie and my best friend Suki clamoured to meet him. 'Not yet,' he told me one afternoon, stroking my cheek. 'All in good time.' Nor had I met any of his friends and family. But it didn't seem to matter, along with the fact he didn't work, although that was OK because neither did I – it was July and we were taking the summer off after A levels.

Logan was my age and the flat belonged to his aunt. I was so busy closing my ears to the concerns of Abbie and my friends they may as well have been made of glass, like those on the mannequin head.

Three weeks to the day of our first date, I jumped off my bike and knocked on Logan's door, weak with the anticipation of him taking me in his arms and feeling his lips on mine. And knocked. And then banged in despair with my fists.

Every fibre of my being told me Logan wasn't simply out.

He'd left my life.

Abbie comforted me as best she could and, to her credit, it was a few days before she said, 'The signs were all there, pet. Everything about Logan screamed that he was keeping you separate from his real life. I'm so sorry.'

Now, clasping my pillow, I wept hard and felt my brittle heart shatter into 100 pieces. Then, drawing breath between sobs, I heard a sound downstairs. Abbie was in bed and the house had been silent.

The noise came again – a kind of clattering.

From the kitchen.

Or – rocking? A heavy item rocking on a wooden surface?

I strained to listen in the darkness, but all was quiet.

Worn out from weeping, I fell asleep.

Dragging myself downstairs next morning, I found Abbie texting rapidly in the kitchen, head bent. She looked up as I entered. 'Hey! Rowena's coming over for dinner tonight. With cake. You look like you need cake.'

'I need shooting,' I sighed. 'But cake will do while I'm building up to it.' Wandering towards the fridge for orange juice, I suddenly remembered the sounds I'd heard from the kitchen last night. As I stood swigging from the plastic bottle, I gazed idly around the room in search of anything that might make a rocking, clattering noise. My eyes came to rest on the glass head and a shudder ran through me.

I had gone to bed after Abbie, gentle snores from her room telling me she'd been fast asleep when I'd tiptoed past.

I'd been the last person in the kitchen and, when I'd put the head down, it had been facing out across the room.

Now it faced the wall.

Seeing my shudder, Abbie remarked, 'Cold, are you? Serves you right for drinking chilled juice straight out of the carton on an autumn morning before the heating comes on!'

For reasons I couldn't explain to myself, I said nothing about the head changing position, instead switching it back to its original place when Abbie trotted out of the room on some errand.

I planned to ask Rowena about it later. And to make sure she took the thing back with her.

When I'd put my hands on the head just now, it was so cold it may as well have been carved from ice. The phrase, 'When hell freezes over' came into my mind and I thrust it straight out, wiping my fingers on my pyjama bottoms with distaste.

It was early evening when I opened the door to a gentle rap from the knocker. Rowena stood on the mat outside, leaf skeletons in dirty brown and orange swirling around her ankle boots in the cool September breeze. Clad in black from her footwear to her velvet frock coat and scarf, she peered up at me through that heavy fringe, the yellow light from the hallway showing her irises to be silver, rather than grey – an eye colour I'd never seen before. That brief, slight narrowing of the eyes again as they met mine before she corrected herself and nodded. 'Lucy.'

I stepped back. 'Come in. We're in the kitchen.' Stamping her feet to get rid of the leaf fragments, Rowena followed me down the hall and I couldn't shake the feeling that she was staring at the back of my head as we walked.

At the kitchen door, Rowena stopped and looked up the stairs. 'I'll just pop to the loo first if that's OK,' she said. I took the proffered cake tin, chatting to my sister until I heard Rowena's tread on the steps as she came down.

In the kitchen, Abbie hugged her new friend while I

stowed her coat on a chair. 'Sit!' she said, pulling out a stool at the island. 'It's only tuna, sweetcorn and pasta salad, I'm afraid, but I like to think our fascinating line in conversation will make up for that. And we can't wait to taste your homemade cake!'

'Abbie adds a special ingredient to the mayonnaise that makes it super-tasty,' I said, taking the seat by Rowena, who looked quickly at me, then away. I frowned. Rowena was in her thirties, so there was no excuse for such poor social skills. She'd barely said a word so far and I couldn't imagine what my bubbly sister saw in her. Then, as our guest's eyes explored the room, she gave a sudden jolt, then seemed to transform into a different person.

'Lucy!' she said, turning towards me. 'I hope you don't mind, but your sister mentioned that your boyfriend disappeared. And that you're really sad.' She patted my hand and I started at the over-familiarity. Yes, I did mind, but it was too late for that. Abbie had clearly told her a while back.

I snatched my hand away and twiddled my fork. 'Logan seemed so loving, so loyal. I didn't have him down as a ghoster.'

'You knew him for three weeks!' retorted Abbie, setting down our steaming bowls. 'He was a stranger.'

Rowena shook her head vigorously as she dipped a spoon into her food, her black bob swirling. 'Time in such matters is irrelevant. When you meet your twin soul, you know immediately. There's a recognition.'

Smiling, I poured water from a jug into our glasses. 'See, Abbie? Logan was my twin soul. Rowena understands.' I shot Rowena a grateful look, but she was staring ahead, motionless. I followed her sight line.

It led to the glass cranium.

Rowena's lips began to move as she spoke in a whisper. 'Pardon?' I said. Ignoring me, she raised her voice. 'What is lost can be found.' She and Abbie exchanged looks and I began to wonder whether the two of them had a secret plan, whether there was more to Rowena visiting than merely to share cake and commiserations.

My answer came after we'd cleared the dinner things away and each enjoyed a slab of our guest's poppy seed cake.

Abbie left the room.

Rowena checked her watch, then faced me. 'Now,' she said with great seriousness, 'we have work to do.' From her bag, she took out two leather draw-string purses and laid them on the marble island. Rising, she lifted the glass head from its place on the bookcase and set it down in front of me. The tiny cauldron was placed by its side, along with a sturdy metal tripod.

'What work?' I asked, beginning to feel alarmed. But I had a sense, somehow, of where this was going.

Abbie returned with two candlesticks from the lounge, set one on either side of the head and lit each with a flaring match. Meanwhile, Rowena emptied the contents of one of the bags, which looked like flakes of greenish plant matter, into the cauldron. From the second, she took a small brown cone and arranged it carefully on the bed of greenery. 'Homemade incense,' she said, 'plus... an extra-special ingredient of my own.' Her nostrils flared as she said 'special' and her hands shook – with fear or excitement, I wondered?

'In a minute,' said Rowena, 'Abbie will dim the lamps and I will light the incense. You, Lucy, will inhale the fragrant smoke as it swirls up to fill the glass head, which I've prepared. In antiquity, a severed head would be used for this purpose, a parchment placed under its tongue bearing words that would command the head to speak. We're a little less barbaric these days' – she gave a nasty laugh – 'but we – humanity – still have questions we can't get answers to by ordinary means. And we have wishes that can't be fulfilled by ordinary means.'

I got to my feet. 'I don't want to do this. Command the head to speak? That sounds wrong. For what purpose? And what does it have to do with me?'

'Despite training since I was a teenager, I just don't have the gift of second sight,' sighed Rowena. 'Yet I can recognise it in others. I saw it in you, that first day we met.'

I snorted. 'Rubbish. I'm not psychic. I'd be aware of it! And I'd know stuff others didn't...'

Abbie spoke up. 'Lucy, you do. So many times you've mentioned things before they happen. You predicted every one of my exam grades – all nine. You knew mum's boyfriend's name years before they met.' She grew sombre. 'And when you were six, you begged Dad not to go out on his motorbike in the snow, telling him he wouldn't come back... I was there. I heard you.'

'That's not fair, reminding me about Dad's death,' I said quietly. Although it had been a long time ago, neither of us could bear to visit his grave, even though the cemetery was within walking distance. 'I can see you're in on this, Abbie. What can you possibly want to know? Or wish for? You have the perfect life – a successful business at 23, the man of your dreams...'

Her face crumpled.

I snapped my fingers. 'Wait – this I do know. You think Dermot's a cheater and that's why he's dragging his feet about the wedding.' She nodded dumbly, a tear squeezing first from the corner of one eye, then the other, before making their way down her cheeks.

'You fight to suppress your intuition, Lucy,' said Rowena. 'To keep it out. It scares you. I can help you make proper use of your gifts.'

An idea formed in my mind and I sat down. 'Tell you what. I'll do it this once – to find out where Logan is. What happened to him. And the story with Dermot. But that's it. I won't do it again. Anyway, what do you want from this, Rowena?'

'The gift. Second sight.' For the first time, she grinned widely, showing undersized, slightly pointed teeth that put me in mind of a creepy porcelain doll I'd seen once in a museum. In the excitement, I'd forgotten how uncomfortable she made me feel. This was a sharp reminder.

'And how will this palaver give you second sight, exactly?' I asked.

As though I hadn't spoken, Abbie reached for the matches. 'Rowena, let's get on with it.' She slid the box over.

Striking a match, Rowena lit the point of the cone in its cauldron bed. As it began to smoulder, she sat the lid on top, then positioned the metal tripod over it. Finally, she balanced the glass head on the tripod. Smoke wafted through the holes in the cauldron's lid and swirled upwards. Gradually the head filled with smoke, which had the effect of making it look more human now you could no longer see through it.

'Shut your eyes, Lucy, and breathe deeply of the scented smoke,' said Rowena. 'Abbie, the lights. Then take one of the books I sent over in the box to note down everything that comes to pass tonight. A record is important.'

My sister jumped from her seat, grabbed a notebook and pen from the side, flicked off the overhead light and sat back down opposite me and Rowena.

One candle illuminated my sister's expectant face, the other our guest's. 'Close your eyes, Lucy, and breathe,' Rowena repeated. 'Breathe in wisdom. I will begin the evocation.'

A thought popped into my head. 'I've seen enough horror films to know we should perform some kind of protection charm before we start–'

'I did that already,' cut in Rowena. 'I surrounded us with white light. Breathe.'

I frowned. I hadn't been aware of her doing this. Still, it seemed I was the one in charge and I needed to know where Logan was. So I dismissed my worry.

Sniffing cautiously, I smelled lavender, thyme and something else – liquorice? Filling my lungs with the scent, I must have spoken out loud. 'Yes,' whispered Rowena. 'Lavender, thyme and myrrh. All good for contacting the dead.' Her whispering continued and grew louder, although I couldn't make out her words.

The dead? That didn't make sense. The smoke

was making me dizzy, disoriented. 'Open your eyes!' commanded Rowena. 'Look into the talking head. What do you see?'

My eyes stinging from the smoke, I drew back, shifting on my stool. Smoke swirled and curled inside the head, which faced me, wearing its usual blank expression. As I watched, to my surprise, pictures formed in the forehead area, moulded from the white, swirling smoke at first. Then the vision shifted and it was like watching a TV screen with colour images.

I gasped. 'Think of what you want to know,' hissed Rowena. 'Then speak of what you see.'

The pictures resolved into recognisable images before I could put my mind into gear. 'A – man. Brown hair, spiked up. On one knee, kneeling. A seashore in the background. Taking out a small box. Holding it out to, to–'

'You're watching Dermot proposing to me?' asked Abbie. 'It was at Eastbourne, on the sand.'

I found I couldn't stop speaking. 'Dermot, yes. Holding the box out to an Indian woman, with long, shiny hair wafting on the sea breeze. They're laughing.'

Abbie let out a sob, flung the pen away and stamped out. I watched the man swing the woman around in an embrace. Then they were gone and it was the white, swirling smoke once more.

'Lucy?' said Rowena. 'That was unfortunate, but keep going, please.'

Giving myself a little shake, I gazed into the mist behind the glass. This time, the picture was closer, panned in. One person, head on a white pillow, pale coils of hair spread out, face in profile. 'It's Logan,' I said, without emotion. A white-coated man blocked my view for a second, then passed behind Logan to adjust – what? 'Logan has a drip in the back of his hand. He's in a hospital bed. His lips cracked, dry – he's really sick.' I strained to see more.

'Where is he?'

'I don't know.' I wanted to feel relief. Logan hadn't simply dumped me, but I seemed to be devoid of feeling in this state. 'Oh – the pictures have gone.'

Rowena wasn't listening. 'This is easier than I expected,' she said. 'You're even more sensitive than I thought. Now it's my turn. I'm going to chant to get some of your powers transferred to me. Keep breathing the incense.'

She began muttering again while I continued to stare into the smoke, unable to look away. Minutes ticked by.

Abbie was back in her seat, both palms on the table, the pen to one side, her face unreadable. I returned my attention to the head. The smoke inside was changing colour, becoming flesh-toned. Inside the glass, hair shot through with grey formed at the top, along with a beard at the chin. Grizzled brows above soft brown eyes. The pouting glass mouth filled up behind with pale pink lips.

A face I hadn't seen for 13 years. My father. His eyes looked into mine and he was speaking, the lips moving silently.

I strained to listen, flooded with feelings at last, my heart banging against my ribs. 'Dad!' I cried desperately. 'I can't hear you!'

Abbie scrambled from her chair and rushed to my side. 'You can see Dad? Where? Show me!'

I pointed a shaking finger.

'There's only smoke. It's not fair. I want to see him too.'

Like a speaker suddenly turned on, Dad's voice came through, shouting inside my head. 'Lucy, you must not do this! You must NOT!'

Abbie tried to push me off the seat to take my place as I reeled back in shock. 'Let me see him!'

Gripping the edge of the table, I fended her off with a sharp elbow. Inside the glass, Dad's eyes were wide, his face contorted. Then the sound of his voice cut out, like a plug in the afterlife had been pulled. My sister gawped. 'What did he say? You look terrified!'

Rowena was grinning again. 'Perfect. The ancestor. I'm starting to see what you see, Lucy. I see a face – misty but getting stronger.'

Suddenly a jigsaw piece slotted into place. 'The ancestor?' I repeated. 'You said something at the start about talking to the dead, Rowena. You wanted my dad to show up?'

'That extra-special ingredient!' she said. 'Lichen, scraped from your dad's gravestone last night at the witching hour. A direct link to him on the astral plane. Evocations are so much more powerful if we can invoke the ancestors. And we did! Too late to stop now. Let's keep going.'

A roar came from Abbie. Snatching up the floor brush, she swept the long handle across the counter top, sending the cauldron and tripod crashing to the ground. The cauldron bounced, its lid flying off and the faintly glowing ashes scattering on the ceramic tiles.

Rather than tumbling onto the marble counter, the head hovered upright in mid-air before coming to rest in front of me neck end first. Smoke curled out, solidifying into a clawed, cadaverous hand which stretched towards my face.

Screaming, I pulled back, batting the thing away. Before it could reach me, the hand became smoke again, drifting upwards and disappearing through the ceiling as the head rolled off the table and shattered on contact with the tiles, shards shooting across the kitchen.

In the pandemonium, I became aware of emotions in the air, hovering around us. Anger. Hatred.

Evil.

Gulping with shock, I watched my sister grab Rowena by her skinny upper arm and drag her into the hall, snatching up her coat on the way. I ran past them to open the front door so Abbie could throw our unwelcome guest out.

'Thanks for a great evening,' Rowena called mockingly from the gate, shrugging on her coat. 'You have my number, Abbie, if you ever need me.'

'Need you? I never want to set eyes on you again!' screamed Abbie, leaning past me to slam the door.

In the kitchen, I held a bin bag open while Abbie swept up the glass and ash, tipping dustpan after dustpan of debris into the sack. We were both silent thinking about the night's revelations when Abbie's phone rang out from the lounge.

My sister was gone for a minute, then returned and held out the handset, her face grim. 'Rowena left a voicemail. Listen.' She pressed a key.

'Message to you both,' came Rowena's triumphant voice. 'You were correct, Lucy – I didn't conduct a protection charm before our evocation. Of course that wasn't going to slip past you. We weren't in my house, so frankly I didn't care what negative entities might be unleashed and anyway, bad energy has its uses. Abbie, you stopped the proceedings before we could wrap up and I could assess the situation. I suspect something was released that needs to be, shall we say, neutralised. I can, if I wish, close things down safely. Sorry to say it, girls, but you *do* need me. Bye for now.'

As Abbie and I exchanged looks, an almighty crash came from the bedroom above us, as though the mahogany wardrobe had been dashed to the floor. That was followed by the bang of the door closing.

'Mum and Dad's room!' we shouted in unison.

Abbie laid a warning hand on my arm. 'We're not going upstairs to see what's happening – this isn't some silly supernatural film. It's real.'

'But we need to work out what to do before whatever it is comes down,' I said. 'How about –' Kneeling on the floor, I put a hand in the bin bag we'd just filled and found the cauldron and tripod. 'Put these back on the counter while I scrape together some crumbs of incense. The head didn't shatter completely. Hopefully there'll be a piece big enough to use.'

Shaking her head, my sister took the items from me and placed them in the sink. 'That's a terrible idea. Rowena is a lunatic but at least she had some idea what she was doing. We don't. We might make things worse.'

Heavy footsteps sounded on the floorboards overhead, walking in the direction of the door. As we listened, the steps paused.

I didn't have to say a word. 'Yep, let's do it,' said Abbie, retrieving the items and arranging them on the counter as Rowena had. She found the candlesticks and slid out a match.

From the floor, I said, 'I've got a few flakes of incense and lichen, but the biggest bit of glass is only two inches long.'

Straightening up, I dropped the flakes into the cauldron and laid the green shard along the tripod, where it promptly fell off, possibly because my fingers were trembling. I felt real terror at the thought that the clawed hand might come for me again. What would it do? I knew the others hadn't witnessed it.

'Surely it doesn't have to be a head, as long as it's transparent?' asked Abbie. 'What's the biggest thing we have that's made of glass?' She dried the water jug with a tea towel and balanced it on the tripod. 'There.' My sister looked anxiously into my face with big eyes.

'Before we start, are we sure we want to do this? Even though we haven't a clue how to go about it?'

I swallowed hard. 'Dead sure. I'm supposed to be the one with the psychic powers out of the three of us. I'll try to shut off my conscious mind and let my subconscious lead the way.'

I took the stool in front of the tripod. Abbie lit the candles, held the lighted match to the sprinkling of incense, shut off the lights and climbed onto the stool next to me. All was peaceful around us. The fragrant smoke began to rise and I inhaled deeply, closing my eyes.

'The jug's filling with smoke,' I heard my sister say. As I braced myself to look, a soft *whumf* from her side caused my lids to spring open. Abbie had slumped forward onto her folded arms. Her face was towards me, eyes shut. 'Abs!' I cried, shaking her shoulder in alarm. 'Wake up! You have to help me!'

Dad's voice inside my head drew my eyes to the jug, his eyes and lips visible within the glass through the mist. 'Sorry, Lucy. You have to do this alone. Your sister is safe there.'

Fear rose in my throat. 'Do what?' I said out loud.

'That girl Rowena planted something upstairs. You must find it and deal with it.'

'But she hasn't been upstairs – oh.' That's why she went straight to the bathroom when she arrived. 'What is it? And where is it?'

'I think I can show you,' said Dad from within my head. 'Take the stairs to my room.' I did so and, reaching the open doorway of the bedroom my parents used to share, I found myself gazing at my father, looking as real and solid as he had last time I'd seen him, before the accident. 'Dad!' I reached out but he dodged my hands, stepping aside so I could enter.

'We don't have much time,' he said, frowning. 'I can only stay as long as the smoke lasts and there was so little grave powder left. In you go. Quickly now.'

I was such a jumble of emotions it was hard to focus. My beloved dad, back. But also dead. The agony of losing him was physical, a squeezing pain in my chest, and I felt myself being dragged back to the horror of the day we found out he was gone...

Dad seemed to read my mind. 'Don't think about that now,' he said. 'Let's start with the wardrobe.'

Although Abbie and I thought we'd heard the

wardrobe fall earlier, it stood in its usual place by the window. The key that normally protruded from the keyhole was gone. I grasped the wooden handles on the front, but it was shut fast. 'Dad?'

'You had the right idea when you said you'd let your subconscious mind guide you,' he replied. 'Use your intuition. Where do you think the key is?'

An image came into my mind. 'The bit of torn carpet under the window. It's under there.' Lifting the flower-patterned corner, I took the key, slotted it in the keyhole and pulled the doors wide. 'What am I looking for?'

'What does your intuition say?'

In my mind's eye, I saw a rat sitting on its haunches. Then, like a speeded-up movie, the rat shut tiny eyes, rolled on its side, stiffened and shrivelled up, its skin turning to parchment. As I watched, the dry skin fell away, leaving the skeleton. Most of that crumbled to dust, leaving just the head. 'A rat's skull,' I said, pushing the few clothes on hangers Mum had left behind to one side so I could peer inside. There, in a corner, sat a small rodent skull. I bent to retrieve it.

'Give it to me,' said Dad eagerly. I turned to look

at him. He seemed animated, impatient, holding my eyes with his and reaching out his palm. My father had been a carpenter, calm, sweet-natured and softly spoken. Something struck me like a thunderbolt and I hit my temple with the heel of my hand.

This was not my dad.

Rowena or whoever had engineered this knew I'd feel such overwhelming emotion and gratitude at seeing my father that I wouldn't question his identity. And now I was in a room with a *thing* pretending to be my dad and it was blocking the doorway. 'What's the matter?' it said, moving closer.

My heart was in my mouth with fear but I had to act normal. I needed to stall. It had said it hadn't much time, only while the grave lichen burned in the cauldron. I had to conceal the fact I knew its secret. But who was this? Was the lichen even from my dad's grave? And what did this thing want with the skull?

The ghostly claw reaching towards me earlier made sense now. My dad wasn't involved at all. Only the malevolent entity.

'Oh, but he was involved,' came a low voice and, as I watched, the rangy figure of my father altered and shrank until I was looking at a short man with sparse black hair and a smooth, round face. 'You've forgotten that I can read your thoughts, although without the rat skull I have no other power apart from to induce sleep in your sister and some minor shape-shifting. Which came in very handy.' He bared his teeth in a loathsome grin.

'The girl Rowena did visit your father's grave yesterday at midnight and scrape off some lichen. But the wind tore the pouch from her hand, blowing it a few feet away. She collected it and returned to the grave for more lichen. But, in the darkness, she found a different grave.

'Mine.

'I was watching – a few of us were – although I had no substance, no body then. But I sensed it was simply a matter of time before I'd be back. And here I am. Mr Ambrose Torreys, most definitely *not* at your service.' The entity gave a mock bow, followed by a high-pitched laugh, like a deranged child.

'The irony is it's me who could be helpful to Rowena because I'd developed skills of prophecy and ritual magic that were coming along beautifully –

that is, until my whore of a wife poisoned me.' He spat at my feet. 'Not that I'd have helped your chum, although she'd have made a useful vessel to inhabit until I worked out how to get a male one. She's gone, but you'll do nicely, my dear.' The man giggled. 'There was so little of your dad's essence in the pot it was easy to elbow him out of the way, so to speak. He had no psychic gifts when alive, so he'd be of limited use if you brought him back. What was he going to do tonight, knock up a couple of kitchen cupboards?'

All the while, the little man was edging closer to me until I was backed up against the window. He made a grab for the skull but I dodged past him and pelted down the stairs to the kitchen. Behind me, Torreys let out a snort of exasperation that began loudly but then cut out.

Abbie still sat at the counter with her head on her folded arms, a tumble of chestnut curls hiding her face. Still with no idea about the significance of the skull, I tucked it out of sight under her armpit and grabbed the nearest leather pouch. The stream of smoke from the incense was thinning to the merest wisp so I had to act fast. My rational mind was horrified by what I planned to do, but my instincts whispered that I was correct.

Turning the pouch inside out, I scraped the lichen fragments lodged in the seams into the cauldron with a fingernail. Miraculously, the other bag had a crumbled bit of incense left so I dropped that in too and tossed in a lighted match.

The smoke gained volume and drifted upwards, quickly filling up the jug and forming features. This time the face *was* my beloved dad. I know because I felt us connect deep within my soul, something that had happened at the start of the first time, before the smoke claw. I'd overridden my sense all wasn't right at the second sitting.

But there was no time for father-daughter bonding. Without hesitating, my Dad said, 'Lucy, that evil man Torreys is here with me. There's more of my grave mould in the cauldron than his now, but we must act fast while I have the upper hand. Wake your sister, take the skull and a hammer, smash it up and bury the bits at the crossroads around the corner. That will neutralise it. Then throw the purses and cauldron in the river where it flows fastest.'

Grabbing a carrier bag, I dug under the sink for the hammer and garden trowel. 'But, Dad, what exactly does the rat skull do?'

'I sense from Torreys that it had a spell put on it many years ago but it was incomplete and needed a particular type of sensitive to awaken its full power,' he replied. 'The relic had to remain hidden in the sensitive's home for two hours to gather strength. Rowena wanted it to make money, but Torrey's wish is to gain influence and get revenge on his wife's descendants. Luckily, Torrey is confined to the room upstairs, where his essence floated to, without the skull. Once the skull and lichen are destroyed, he'll go back where he came from.'

Dad's voice grew fainter. 'Now wake Abbie!' In the glass, the smoke was fading along with his face. 'Dad, don't go!' I pleaded. 'Leave the jug, like Ambrose Torrey did, so we can hang out!'

'I can't materialise like him. Anyway, that would be wrong. It's unnatural. I'll visit you and your sister in your dreams when I can. And make sure you come to visit me. I love you and Abbie, my dear, dear girls. Remember that. Remember me.' And he was gone.

Tears streaming down my cheeks, I shook my sister's shoulders roughly. 'Hey!' she said groggily, rubbing her eyes with her knuckles. She looked at me sharply, then around the table. 'Why are you crying? And what's this under my arm?' She held up the skull.

Gabbling about what she'd missed, I threw the skull and other items in the bag, then dragged Abbie to the hall to get our coats. She chuckled. 'You've lost your mind. I don't believe a word of it, but Rowena was clearly nuts, so let's pop to the roundabout on Castle Road – that's a crossroads – and bury our animal skull if it makes you feel better. If we come home via Castle Bridge, we can drop the rest of the stuff over the side into the river.'

That's what we did, and if any passing motorists were startled at the sight of two girls digging in the middle of a roundabout at midnight, they didn't bother to stop and ask what we were up to. Luckily.

When I finally fell into bed, exhausted, I did dream about Dad. I was grown up and we walked along the sunlit path by the caravan park we used to visit on family holidays, my arm through his, and chatted. I forget what about, as you do with dreams, but that doesn't matter. Waking up, I felt less alone than I had in years. In the morning, Abbie said she'd had that dream too.

She dumped Dermot and, although I found out Logan had been in a serious cycling accident and transferred to Wales to be near family, I didn't want to be in a relationship with him. It was time to look forwards, not backwards, and I took a job as a teaching assistant in readiness to take up my place at teacher training college the following September.

And although Mum and Dad's room seemed safe, Abbie and I read up on spiritual cleansing and burnt a sage stick in there to clear out any bad energy.

We visit Dad's grave every month. The first time, after I'd placed a vase of yellow chrysanthemums before the headstone, we'd hugged hard and agreed we'd been fortunate to have him on Earth with us, even for such a short time.

Threading our way through the graves on the way to the wooden gate that led out, my sister and I passed a headstone that we both glanced at. *Ambrose Torreys*, it read in faded stencilling, *1911-1955*. Neither of us remarked on it.

FIVE

NIPPER

THE LAST THING YOU want on a frosty Christmas Eve is to reach the station and discover your connecting train's been cancelled.

Gina stepped off the light, bright train onto the dismal platform and her heart dropped. A waiting room with a large window was the main source of illumination in the darkened station, both ends of the platform disappearing into blackness.

The carriage she'd left had been filled with groups, couples and singletons like her on their way, she imagined, to fun festive gatherings, although she wouldn't describe her destination as such. The table to her right had held four youths in their twenties, wearing Santa hats and belting out Christmas songs.

As she wondered whether she dared ask them to tone it down, a mum, dad and their young son had clattered onto her table, covering the top with comics, toys and snacks.

This was the last straw. But seeing how loving the family were to each other and how warmly the father had responded when she'd asked them to mind her seat while she braved the rocking aisles to buy tea, she found herself relaxing and able to ignore the rowdy lads.

The boy was around six years old, like her stepbrother, Joel, and chatting to the child about nursery and his Lego model made her feel more cheerful, or at least less apprehensive, at the thought of her first Christmas as a blended family. Gina wanted to get it over with and get back to her real life. From its first day, 2022 would be different to this year. Hopefully Covid would be defeated. She'd leave her supermarket manager job and become an estate agent. She'd find a new boyfriend. And she'd finally decide whether to grow her hair or chop the whole annoying lot off.

Gina had caught the train from Manchester Piccadilly and was changing at Mournsteadham, a tiny station, to finish the last leg to her mother and stepdad's new house in Durfall village. Her elder brother Stephen was driving up from Devon with his kids, and Gina looked forward to seeing them, at least.

Plonking her heavy holdall by her feet, she looked up and down the short platform, lit by three lampposts at regular intervals.

A low fence ran the platform's length, the bushes and trees behind stretching away into the gloom. In the centre squatted a small, old-fashioned waiting room in honey brick with a bench outside. The exit was signposted some way down the platform. Across the tracks was the same fence, waiting room and lights.

Pleased with herself, Gina had arrived with 15 minutes to spare before her train so she wouldn't be hanging around the station long.

This had been a mistake.

Above her, the departure board showed her train, the 19:16 to Durfall, had been cancelled. 'What? No!' she exclaimed out loud. The train due in 10 minutes was no use to her but the display promised the next one to Durfall at 20:00. 'That's nearly 45 minutes,' she thought, kicking her bag in fury, 'an hour from now. I may have frozen to death by then.' Still, at least she had her novel and phone.

Plucking her phone from her coat pocket, she texted her mum the news. *Keep warm, darling, and we'll see you when we see you*, replied her mother. *Can't wait! The mulled wine is waiting XX.*

Typically upbeat, but not saying what Gina really wanted to hear: that someone would drive the hour or so to collect her rather than leaving her in this fridge of a place.

Maybe she could get a cab? Having never made the journey before, Gina had no idea where Mournsteadham station was in relation to the town centre, if indeed there was one. It seemed unlikely there'd be a taxi place outside, like the station at home.

With so much time to kill, Gina wandered down the platform the way her train had come. The skeleton of a beech tree overhung the fence and a white line ran the length of the platform edge. At the end, a slatted metal fence topped with spikes and several signs attached barred her way. *Danger! Do not touch the live rail!* screamed one, illustrated by a black lethal-looking lightning arrow in a yellow triangle. Beyond was in shadow, then total darkness.

As she turned to stroll to the other end, something streaked past her feet, making her jump back. A plump grey rat slithered up the fence in front of her, dropping over the other side into the gloom. Alarmed to find herself close to the platform edge, Gina was about to head towards the middle when movement on the opposite platform caught her eye.

Across from her stood a thin man in light coloured trousers. Then the air seemed to shift and she found herself looking at a poster, half-hidden by a lamppost, that gave the impression of a figure. Unsettled, she continued on her way.

The platform's top end had the same fence and signs, the two sets of train tracks disappearing into the yawning black mouth of a tunnel.

A quick look outside the exit confirmed there was no taxi rank. Gina's hands were growing numb inside her gloves so she made for the waiting room, grateful there was at least some shelter from the biting cold.

The room was narrow, with a bank of plastic moulded seats, each separate with curved edges to discourage rough sleepers, she assumed.

It contained one traveller, a middle-aged woman

with a headful of blonde plaits attached to grey, frizzy afro roots. She smiled and adjusted her glasses on her nose as Gina entered. 'Come in, child, come in,' she said, as though inviting Gina into her own front room. 'I'd say come out of the cold, but it's no warmer in here.' She gave a phlegmy chuckle followed by a cough as Gina sat down two seats away, idly wondering why the woman hadn't either dyed her natural hair to match the extensions or had grey plaits fitted instead.

'You been abandoned by your family too?' the woman remarked, producing an orange bobble hat and pulling it over her hair. 'People stuck outdoors this time o' night on Christmas Eve don't have many who care for them.' Gina was indignant. 'My family cares. They're busy getting the house ready for visitors,' she said. 'Otherwise they'd collect me.' The woman's words felt too close to the truth, but she wasn't about to discuss her concerns with a stranger. Her mother and stepfather had no doubt both already had one too many sherries to take to the wheel.

'If you say so, child. My daughter's invited me over, but I wouldn't be surprised if she's forgotten now she has that new man. No time for me, the woman who raised her, anymore.' Again, too near to Gina's position for comfort.

After her parents' divorce seven years ago, when she was 14, her dad had moved to Palm Springs with his new wife, found within weeks on a dating site, while her mother had shacked up with Colin, the man who'd been more important than her marriage and led to its breakdown. Gina and her brother had been an inconvenience to her mother as she forged her new life, which soon included a new baby, and before they left home as adults, Gina and Stephen had spent Christmases with their gran.

This conversation wasn't exactly filling her with Christmas cheer, so Gina was relieved when the woman glanced at her phone and got to her feet, leaning heavily on a walking stick. 'My train will be here in a minute and I hope yours is on time,' she said with a smile.

As she passed, she plucked the bobble hat from her head and plonked it on Gina's. 'You've still got a while. Pull that over your ears. Happy Christmas, child.' Gina wished her the same and the woman paused at the doorway, concern in her eyes. Turning, she said something over her shoulder that sounded like, 'Watch out, it can get very nippy' but kept walking and her words were drowned out by the train screeching into the station. 'Pardon?' called Gina. But the woman was out of earshot, hauling herself up the train steps with the handrails. Then with a clatter and a scream, the train vanished into the night.

Oh well. The hat will help a little, Gina thought, dragging it down over her chilly ears, her curly bobbed hair sticking out at the bottom.

She couldn't see the departure board from the waiting room, so ventured out to check her train hadn't been cancelled. There it was: next train to Durfall, 20:00. Phew!

As she stood looking at the display, a small cotton handkerchief blew over, dancing around her ankles before drifting away and disappearing onto the tracks.

Litter louts, her mum would say. Why don't people use the bins? One was attached to the lamppost near her, a metal hoop with a transparent bag, coffee cups visible in the bottom. Although maybe litter louts don't use cloth hankies, she thought, ducking back into the waiting room. Then it struck her. The night was still, windless. So why was litter blowing about? She chided herself, laughing. What idiot would be unsettled by a handkerchief?

Gina closed the metal-framed door and settled on a chill plastic seat. Taking her novel from the holdall, she opened it on her knee, keen to distract herself for the remaining 45 minutes. She favoured 'women in peril' thrillers, typically with a muddy green or blue cover depicting a female figure from the back. Normally she could lose herself in one of these. Tonight, in the middle of nowhere, she found she didn't want to dwell on the harm that might befall a lone woman.

As she stowed the book in her bag, planning to swop it for the frothy charm of a woman's magazine, she felt a sharp sensation on the side of her neck, like a sting from a large insect. 'Ouch!' she cried, rubbing the spot with her fingers. Her eyes roamed the room in search of the creature that had stung her, but there were no insects in sight. Hardly the season for bees or wasps.

Then she spotted something white on the floor, not far from her foot. Another small handkerchief, opened out in a square this time. A woman's. How odd! Maybe someone bought a packet for their gran's Christmas present and instead decided to open it and throw the contents around the station. As you might do if you were a litter lout. Although, she mused, being close enough to see the piece of cotton properly, it wasn't the crisp white of a new handkerchief. It was slightly yellowish, as though it had been washed plenty of times, and was crumpled, as from a pocket. In the corner was an 'S', embroidered in pink chain stitch. 'Well, S, I hope you're having a better Christmas than I am,' she said to it.

Noticing the door was ajar, Gina rose to close it, sliding the handle home firmly so it would stay shut. As she turned to go back to her seat, she felt a painful sting on the other side of her neck, again clapping her hand to the spot. This time, she realised what the sensation reminded her of. As a girl, when she'd thought she was part of a happy family, she'd owned a Jack Russell, Tovey. Tovey had long since departed for the great boneyard in the sky, but when she threw a tennis ball for him in the garden, he'd get overexcited, yapping madly and darting forward to nip her calves with his teeth.

She laughed uneasily. Obviously there was no dog here. But what was – there was only one word for it – *attacking* her? Gina stood in the centre of the room. In front of her was the window overlooking the platform.

What a sight I am, she thought. I so need a bath and a hair wash. In the glass, her locks stuck out from under the hat in a brown frill, her nose glowing from the cold, the padded collar of her khaki coat sticking up. Then her image faded, replaced by – what *was* that? A mouth? Yes, a young man's, with the shadow of a moustache above thick, mobile lips, closed at first, then drawing back into a grimace that widened as though in a silent, agonised cry, showing short teeth with an expanse of gum. Then the teeth were bathed in red and the mouth widened into a silent scream before bringing the bared bloody teeth together with a snap she couldn't hear. The monstrous, disembodied mouth put her in mind of the Cheshire Cat's grin in *Through The Looking Glass*, hanging in the air without a face.

Then the image was gone and it was just her

features, eyes wide with horror. Before she could move away, she felt a searing pain on her cheek. It felt like a set of teeth had sunk into her flesh and clamped together powerfully before letting go. There was no mistaking that. She'd been bitten viciously. But by what? The teeth disappeared but the pain remained as she rubbed the skin hard in an effort to confuse the nerve endings and disperse the sensation.

Too shocked even to scream, she darted to the seat and grabbed her holdall. Then the handkerchief was under her feet and she slipped, landing on one knee on the tiles and letting out a yelp of pain. It was hard to put her weight on that leg but she wasn't staying an instant longer.

Would the man let her leave?

Whimpering, she made for the door and hauled it open. Her eye caught the lettering of the departure board clock: 19:55. The train was due in five minutes but she had to escape.

Lifting her bag to her shoulder, she approached the exit, pulling out her phone to call her mother. Too late, she saw the handkerchief – and she assumed it had been the same one all along – as it tangled around her boot, causing her to stumble. The phone flew from her hand, landing on the edge of the platform. She stooped to retrieve it just as it slid off onto the tracks, as though nudged by an invisible foot. And there it would have to stay.

Catching her breath, she staggered towards the gate, praying it hadn't somehow been locked. Oh joy – it was open! She swung it outwards and found herself on a woodland pathway. With just a few streetlights at such long intervals it was largely in darkness, normally she would have avoided the path at this time on a winter's night. Today she had no choice but to start off down it.

She made her way along the dirt path, hypervigilant to the sounds around her. A few yards in, she heard her train arrive and depart. No one appeared to get off. Gina was too far away to run to catch it, even without a painful leg.

There must be a highway of some sort, but where? It couldn't be far. Every few feet, she turned to make sure she was alone.

After 10 minutes, she almost sobbed with relief as she rounded a bend and spotted a road 70 yards away.

A car flashed past, the strains of Slade's *Merry Xmas Everybody* floating out. Not so merry from where I am, Gina thought bitterly.

She limped the last few feet, noting her leg was less sore and that she could probably walk normally. Resting her hand on a tree trunk, Gina straightened up, stretching her denim-clad leg out to test it, flexing the knee a few times. 'Yep – fine,' she thought – then she saw a figure in between her and the road.

A man, tall, dressed in a shiny black leather biker's jacket and cream trousers, dark eyes on hers and with that obscene, mobile mouth she recognised from the station. Was this the chap she'd seen on the opposite platform too? He wore a stricken expression and Gina stayed where she was. Then the man began to shudder, his head bobbing as though he were on a juddering machine, such as an engine. As she watched, his head twitched, then jerked sharply to one side, the eyes suddenly unseeing, and the back of his head exploded, blood, flesh and shards of bone spraying the bushes on either side. The jaw clenched, then dropped as the rest of his face fell away, leaving that familiar bloody grimace, but attached to the body by strips of skin that were the remnants of his chin and neck, along with a splinter of spinal cord. Then the man vanished as her muscles unlocked and she fled screaming past where he'd stood and out onto the road.

There was no pavement, just the road with grassy banks and bushes on either side. Leaving the dimly lit path, she plunged into total blackness as far as she could see but pelted along blindly, tears streaming down her face, with no idea where she was going. Her knee began to twinge again and she was soon out of breath. Thank goodness it was only a few minutes before she saw lights ahead.

A pub?

Set back from the road, a whitewashed building whose dangling sign declared its name to be *The Blackened Boar* reared up in front of her, a few cars visible outside.

As she charged through the door, the scene from *An American Werewolf In London* flashed into her mind, where a pair of backpackers walk into an isolated pub on the Yorkshire moors and the hostile locals turn to glower. And there's a pentagram painted on the wall.

Not surprisingly, given how noisily she'd entered, several customers did glance up but, after studying her for a few seconds and dismissing her as uninteresting, went back to their drinks and conversations. The cream walls, tobacco-stained despite indoor smoking having been banned for over a decade were, thankfully, pentagram-free.

The room, of medium size, smelled of stale beer and damp but she could also detect the aroma of fresh coffee. Approaching the bar, Gina threw her holdall on one stool and hitched herself onto another before resting her elbows on the counter and leaning over in search of staff. A glance in the mirrored wall behind the bar showed her panting and wild-eyed, her hat having ridden up to the top of her head, bobble drooping to one side. The overall effect was, she imagined, that of an escaped lunatic.

From the bar's back room, a woman with heavily rouged cheeks and thin pencilled brows appeared. 'You look like you need a stiff one, love,' she said, holding up a spirit glass. 'Car broke down? You far from home?'

A man with thinning, sandy hair slipped onto the

stool by Gina, his arm nudging hers on the bar. 'It's on me, Zosia,' he said, blinking pale, hooded eyes at the barmaid. 'Whatever the lady wants.'

Gina couldn't believe someone was hitting on her when it must have been clear to even the most stupid person that she was in a terrible state. She didn't normally drink spirits, but tonight she was cold to the marrow, not to mention in shock. Ignoring the man, she said, 'A double whiskey, please. And I'd love a coffee, if you have any?'

'And I'm buying,' said the man.

Gina opened her mouth to protest, but the woman said, 'You don't need to worry, love. Simon is one of the good guys. He's our local copper, PC Ankers. He's here because his wife had a C-section two days ago and is in hospital.'

'Bringing our daughter home tomorrow – Christmas Day,' he beamed. 'Our first. We've called her Ivana. My wife is Russian.'

The man held up broad hands. 'I'm harmless, honest. Just a bit lonely tonight without my wife. And I'm even happy to make a tit of myself in this Christmas jumper so folk will talk to me.' He pointed to the forlorn-looking Rudolph with a wobbly red pom-pom nose on his navy top and Gina laughed for the first time in hours.

Her drinks arrived along with a bottle of beer for Simon. She tipped the whiskey into the coffee and took a sip, cradling her hot beverage between her hands. They were still too cold for her to take off her gloves.

'So your car's had it,' said Simon kindly. 'Where are you trying to get to?'

'My mum's, in Durfall.' Gina stirred her drink with the spoon sitting in her saucer. 'And I'm not in a car – I can't drive. I've come from the station.' She turned to face Simon fully for the first time and he gasped. He was staring at her cheek and, self-consciously, she raised her fingers to the area and winced. It was bruised and tender, and she could feel indentations in two semi-circular rows. To her surprise, Simon slid from his seat, collected his beer and nodded in the direction of an empty table in the corner, indicating that she should follow.

They sat down. Above their heads, Jona Lewie's *Stop The Cavalry* rang out and a group on the next table joined in, giggling and making parping sounds to imitate the trombone chorus.

'Your face,' he said, leaning towards her. 'You've been bitten.'

It was a statement, not a question.

Gina placed her hat on the table and wound a strand of hair around her index finger, as she did when she was nervous.

'Those are human teeth marks,' he continued. 'And you've come from the station. Your accent tells me you're not from around here. So you don't know the story.'

Unable to think of anything to say, she shook her head, dipping it to take a drink.

'My dad was a copper too, in his early twenties in the 1970s when there was a scandal in the village. Young lad by the name of Mackenzie was having an affair with a married woman, Sophia.

'The lad's 25th birthday was Christmas Eve and she'd promised to leave her husband on that day in 1971, so they could spend Christmas together and, he thought, the rest of their lives. They arranged to meet at the station to catch the train to Edinburgh.

'Mackenzie was so excited he got to the station an hour early so was in the waiting room when Sophia arrived soon after – with her husband. They saw Mackenzie and there was a fight. Sophia's husband punched the boy and she later said she'd yelled at him that the affair was over for good. Then Sophia and her husband boarded the inter-city train.

'Mackenzie climbed onto the tracks in the tunnel, hiding until he heard the next train. Then he put his neck on the rail and – well, you can imagine. My dad was one of the attending officers and he told me the details when I started my training.

'Dad's retired but he mentions it sometimes – said it was one of the most terrible things he's ever seen, the head burst apart at the back like a smashed melon, with just the boy's face left. A bit of his face, to be exact. Just his mouth and jaw, stretched wide in a scream and attached to his body by a few strips of skin. Perhaps he changed his mind as the train came thundering towards him and tried to get up, given that it didn't run over his whole head.

'Sophia must have dropped her hanky because one was found in the lad's hand with her initial in the corner.

'She and her husband moved away in the New Year. So did Mackenzie's family.'

Simon paused. 'Then, 25 years later on Christmas Eve, a young woman was bitten on the face at the station and swore she saw him. Or saw his mouth, at least, in the waiting room window. The situation isn't funny, I know, but you need gallows humour in our job.' He gave a wry smile. 'Dad said after that, they nicknamed the dead lad Mac the Nipper.

'We've heard nothing of him since. But it's 2021 – exactly 50 years tonight since his death. I don't believe in ghosts. Not in my job, with the things I've seen.

'But maybe you were the right age, in the wrong place at the wrong time, and he attacked you. I guess he's still angry at Sophia and takes it out on women every quarter of a century.'

Gina was speechless, remembering the words of the woman in the waiting room. Rather than warning her about the cold, had she actually said something like, 'Watch out for the Nipper'?

'Tell you what,' said Simon. 'Why don't I drive you to your mum's? The 8pm train was the last to Durfall.

It's not like I have anything better to do tonight. You'd struggle to get a cab anyway around here.'

Gina found her voice at last. 'That would be incredibly kind of you,' she managed. 'I lost my phone at the station so I can't even tell Mum I'm stranded.'

Simon got to his feet. 'I'll grab us a couple of Zosia's turkey sandwiches, then we can get going.'

He returned with two foil-wrapped packages and led Gina outside to his car. She settled into the white Peugeot's passenger seat, pulling the seatbelt across to buckle it while Simon fired up the heater. 'There you go,' he said, handing her a pack of sandwiches. The next minute, Gina was opening her dinner while Simon checked the road before edging out, so neither saw the mobile mouth with its bloody grin in the car's rear-view mirror.

SIX

THE ANCESTRAL SEAT

THE RENOVATIONS SEEMED TO go on forever, so Ella and I could hardly believe they were over as we showed the last workman out of our newly gloss-painted front door.

'I never want to see another plumber as long as I live!' she exclaimed, then squealed as I caught her around the waist and carried her to the front room, her legs kicking like a toddler's. I fell on the sofa, pulling her onto my lap. 'In that case, you can change the washers if the taps leak, my love,' I said into her hair before planting a kiss on her ear.

'They won't! Well, nothing should go wrong for a good while. We have the perfect house. We certainly paid enough to make it perfect!' She patted my cheek, then scrambled to her feet.

'Hey, Mrs Wilkins, watch those heels on the sanded

floor,' I mock scolded. 'The varnish is only just dry. We need a huge rug – and a bit more furniture than a sofa in here.'

I pointed to the corner by the bay window. 'You know what would work well there? A club chair – one of those antique brown leather ones. Something lived-in, super comfy–'

'Softened by a century of other people's bums – how weird!' laughed Ella, one dimple sinking into her cheek in the way I loved. Slipping off her work shoes and leaving them on their sides, soles together, she padded over to the window and looked out. 'On the street of our dreams at last! It was worth hanging round the auction houses for three years waiting for the right doer-upper. Even though we both have stress-induced grey hairs after eight months of dust and hammer-bangers.' She picked up a skein of her wavy brown hair and pretended to tut at it. Then she turned back to me, her face softening. 'We're pretty much cleaned out financially, but I know how important it is to you to have one of those chairs. You've brought it up a few times. It can go on the credit card.'

I swallowed hard, swallowed the sadness down so she wouldn't see. My childhood hadn't been happy – correction, it had been bearable so long as my dad had been alive. His death when I was nine hit the family hard as Mum didn't have a profession as such. Then, without Dad to pay the bills and to take her anger at the world out on, it was me who was hit hard whenever life got too much for her. And when Mum's criticism and yelling got too much for me, I'd take my yellow rabbit and sit in dad's brown leather chair by the window, legs dangling as the deep seat meant I couldn't reach the floor. I felt his presence there, comforting and warming me against her coldness like the sun.

Until I came home from school one day before the Easter holidays, singing to myself and looking forward to settling in Dad's chair with a buttered hot cross bun to watch cartoons.

I stopped short in the living room doorway. There, in Dad's corner, was a moss-green velvet chair with a row of tassels dangling from under the arms. In it sat my mother, who lifted a teacup to her lips theatrically when she saw me. She normally didn't go near Dad's chair, let alone sit in it.

'What?' she said, feigning innocence at my shocked face. 'That chair was ancient and scruffy with greasy arms. Harry next door took it to the dump. This chair's much nicer. Don't you think?'

Harry next door. I may have been a kid, but I knew what Mum had got up to with our neighbour when Dad was at the hospital having chemo, trying to stay alive to look after his little family. I spotted them through our kitchen window. You could see into Harry's kitchen from ours. My mother, against the sink with her skirt up around her waist and old Harry between her legs.

'That was all I had of my dad!' I yelled, stamping my foot and throwing my schoolbag to the floor. My maths and English exercise books spilled out. 'How could you!'

Mum simply smirked and sipped her tea.

'Your dad is gone. I'm still here. *We're* still here. We need to move on and that chair keeps you thinking about your dad. It's not healthy. So I got rid of it. For your sake.'

I ran upstairs sobbing. Mum didn't follow. She

always left me to cry alone, to 'cry it out', as she called it. Now I call her behaviour by its real name: neglect. Not to mention cruelty.

It felt as though I'd lost Dad all over again.

Today, I said quietly, 'I'm touched that you remembered about Dad's chair, Ell. That means a lot.'

A fortnight later, I came in from work to find the situation from that April afternoon with my mother in reverse.

Ella and I were firm believers in upcycling and her friend Sara had given us a blue patterned rug to clothe the bare floor, lending a cosiness to the room. We'd added a large TV on a stand. And there by the window sat a chair in chestnut brown leather with scrolled arms and a fat cushioned seat. The rug didn't reach as far as the chair, but it looked very at home with its bun feet resting on the honey-coloured floorboards.

You might not think a chair could make a grown man cry. Well, this chair did.

Ella came in from the kitchen and I hastily wiped my tears on my cuff before she could see. 'I didn't know exactly what your dad's chair looked like, but you said brown leather club, so I thought this would probably do,' she said, stroking one of its cracked arms before hugging me. 'There wasn't room in the flat, so how great is this that we can finally get the things we want around us? I'd had my eye on this specimen in that house clearance place behind the supermarket. And here it is!'

I hugged her back. 'I love it. And I love you for finding it.'

My wife gave me her dimpled grin again. 'Hey, John, get that cute butt of yours over here.' She patted the chair seat with a smile.

I took two steps towards it and eased myself down, stretching my arms along the chair's leather arms. It felt right, so comfortable. I fitted into the chair as though it were made for me.

Half an hour later, I grabbed a book from work, dragged over one of our side tables and positioned it within easy reach of my new throne. Then I settled down to read with a coffee. Bliss.

That evening, Ella and I sat on the sofa to watch TV with dinner on our laps on trays, as we normally did at the end of the day. Creatures of habit, we liked to sit in the dim light from the floor lamp behind us as part of our wind-down-for-bed routine.

I found my gaze drawn to the leather chair from time to time, such as during ad breaks in our TV shows. Looking at it gave me a warm feeling. I sighed with contentment.

I wasn't exactly picturing my dad in the chair, but it simply being in the room made me feel closer to him. He'd died suddenly and I hadn't got to say goodbye – a source of enormous sadness. Mum had known Dad was dying but thought it would upset me to see him as wasted as he'd become in his last weeks. No, Mum, I remembered bitterly. Far less distressing to a child to be allowed to hug and kiss his dad and say a proper farewell, rather than his last meeting with his father being when the man was laid out in a coffin in the church.

I turned my thoughts back to the TV. It was coming up to 10pm, and Ella and I rationed our news-watching to three times a week because it was usually so depressing it dragged our mood right down. The *News At Ten* theme tune began.

'I can't take mad politicians, price rises and murders today, J,' said Ella, shaking her head. 'I have an early meeting tomorrow, so I'll go and read myself to sleep with my nice, gentle novel. Don't wake me when you come up.'

At 11 o'clock, I switched off the TV, took our trays into the kitchen and popped back to turn off the lounge lamp. Walking in, I thought I saw a long shadow fall across the brown chair but, as I stared, there was nothing there. Silly, I said to myself as I climbed the stairs to our bedroom.

I could see into the lounge from my position on the stairs and, on a whim, I looked over. The room was in darkness, the chair visible in the light from the hallway. The shadows seemed particularly dense on the chair back, seat and along the arms. It was as though someone were reclining in the chair in the same position I'd taken up when I first sat in it. Then the shadow faded. My imagination, obviously.

Next morning, I got the bus to my office. Ella had already left.

Switching off my computer at the end of the day, I found I was looking forward to coming home to see the chair rather than my wife! Most peculiar. And indeed, there it was, squatting in its corner, which made me smile. But I felt that things were somehow different. What had changed?

I stood in the doorway, stroking my chin and frowning.

'You know what would make the place feel even cosier?' Ella had come in through the front door behind me. She slammed it shut. 'Cushions, piles of squashy cushions. Our new sofa is cool, but the back's a bit stiff. Cushions would make all the difference.'

'What is it with women and cushions?' I said, laughing. 'Blokes never think about these things.'

'Well, your back will thank me,' said Ella. 'I fancy some second-hand cushions. With character.'

'Cushions of distinction. Now there's a phrase,' I chuckled, throwing my jacket at her, which she caught, giggling.

'I think I spotted cushions at the house clearance place. Let's go cushion-hunting tomorrow,' she said, hanging our coats up in the hall.

Next day was a Saturday. We had scrambled eggs on toast at the local café, then strolled down the high street to our destination.

A gent in his sixties with a frill of white hair and sharp cheekbones sat at a knick-knack filled glass case that doubled as a desk by the shop entrance, poring over a weekend broadsheet newspaper. The space was huge and among the desks, jugs, grandfather clocks and other junk-shop paraphernalia were a couple of tastefully arranged room sets. In one, a burgundy leather Chesterfield had a range of cushions along the back. Ella headed straight over.

'Oh, I love this!' she exclaimed, reaching for a red cushion bearing an appliquéd lady in a crinoline and pressing it to her cheek. 'And these three.' She pointed to two cream cushions embroidered with peacocks, and a mushroom linen one with a flower and foliage pattern. 'One of those either side of the sofa and the red one in the middle. The mushroom one's just right for your chair.'

Scenting a sale, the shop owner came over. 'They're a job lot from the same house,' he said in sonorous, actorly tones, fixing us with navy blue eyes. 'We got quite a few items from there. The cushions date from the 1920s, I believe. They've seen some wear and tear, so you can have all four for £30 if you want them.'

There was something peculiar about the mushroom cushion. The embroidered leaves and flowers seemed to swim before my eyes. Feeling dizzy, I blinked twice to clear my head, keeping my eyes shut a fraction longer than necessary the second time. Opening them, the sensation had gone.

'Maybe not the mushroom one, love,' I said, feeling foolish.

'They're beautiful antiques and I want them all,' said Ella petulantly, fishing in her purse for three £10 notes, which she pressed into the shop owner's hand. 'I'll hide the mushroom one in the spare room if it bothers you,' she whispered, nudging me in the ribs.

Now it was the shopkeeper's turn to whisper. 'Never underestimate the fairer sex's love for soft furnishings,' he said from behind his hand, winking as Ella gently packed them into the bags she'd brought specially. I smiled to myself. Of the two of us, I was the sentimental one. Ella and I had met five years ago at the bank where she'd smashed through so many glass ceilings, I was surprised she didn't have a permanent headache. I'd come in on a contract to fiddle with the company's client database and been mesmerised by this ballsy beauty of a team leader who took shit from no one. Me included.

I did battle with the Saturday supermarket crowds while Ella transported her squashy treasures back to the house.

Coming in 40 minutes later, I walked past the lounge on the way to the kitchen, dumping the carrier bags on the table. From upstairs, the sound of splashing and humming told me Ella was having a bath. Hearing the door shut behind me, she called, 'I've just got in and I'm planning a good soak. See you in an hour!'

I made myself a ham sandwich and carried it through to the lounge with a glass of fresh lemonade. I'd recorded a football game and wanted to take advantage of Ella's temporary absence to watch some of it. Three of her new old cushions sat along the back of the sofa, a cream one at either end and the red one in the centre.

With a start, I saw that despite her promise, Ella had placed the mushroom cushion on my chair. Although the object looked quite ordinary, something about it bothered me. I knew I should break the spell by picking it up, but I couldn't bring myself to touch it. Instead, I went past it to the sofa.

Switching on the TV, I sat down, tucked the middle cushion behind me and settled back to eat my lunch, focusing on the football.

I managed to get to half-time before Ella wandered in, a towel wrapped around her held up under the arms, damp hair plastered back from her forehead and a big grin on her face. I swept breadcrumbs from my jeans as she perched on the edge of the sofa. 'See! You're enjoying the cushions. And the mushroom one looks adorable on your chair, so let's leave it. I'll protect you from it.'

I open my mouth to reply, then shut it again. To the side of her, I could see my chair. The mushroom cushion, which had sat squarely along the seat, was now propped up at one side with a corner sticking up. I shook my head. Maybe I hadn't taken its position in properly.

'What's up?' asked Ella. 'You're scowling.'

'I was thinking about the extra work I need to do,' I lied. 'I just had a text from my boss saying there was something that absolutely had to be completed today. I know it's a Saturday and you and I were going to visit that park we spotted, so I'm really sorry. How about we go tomorrow?'

It was true I'd had a text from my boss, but that wasn't worrying me. I felt troubled and needed to distract myself with a complex, engrossing problem.

'That's OK,' sighed Ella, rubbing at her hair with a hand towel. 'Megan texted earlier to see if I was up for a stroll this afternoon. It's only 12pm – not too late to contact her. I'll get straight on it.'

As she went upstairs to change, the cushion caught my eye again. With its pointed top, the body of the cushion was collapsed forward on itself, the embroidered flowers coming together in a most unsettling arrangement. It looked like a face, an elderly, malevolent male face with heavy brows and a disdainfully curled upper lip, the outer folds of the cushion forming plump cheeks. The features seemed oddly familiar.

That was it. Heart banging, I leaped to my feet and picked up the cushion, punching and shaking it. Immediately the face was gone, the stitches back in their pattern of flowers and leaves.

Absolutely ridiculous. Who ever heard of a malevolent cushion?

Later that afternoon, typing away rapidly on my laptop in the study we shared upstairs, I got a text from Ella asking what time I'd be finished.

Sorry, babe, I replied. *Gavin's relying on me to sort out this bug in the programme for our new client. This evening's a write-off. Is Megan free for dinner? It's on me X.*

We both had friends within walking distance, one of the other attractions of this area. I groaned at the thought of an evening in front of my laptop, but soon got so absorbed in teasing out the errors in the programme that the hours flew by. The intricacies of computing may be boring to most, but as a lonely, geeky kid, the machines had been my salvation after Dad died. No wonder I'd made working with them my profession.

The room grew darker, the only light coming from the anglepoise lamp on the corner of my desk, pulled low to highlight my notes, along with the ghostly white glow from my screen that lit up my keyboard.

Close to a solution to the problem, my fingers flew over the keys as shadows gathered in the corners of the room, the space under the guest bed at my elbow black and dense. No other lights were on in the house as I hadn't left my seat for – I checked the digital display at the bottom of my screen – five hours! It was 21:45. My fingers aching, I shook my hands out, then arched my back, kneading my waist with my knuckles. Time for tea! Decaff, though, so I didn't spend the night staring at the ceiling.

Pushing myself away from the desk on my office chair's wheels, I froze.

Downstairs, someone was walking across the lounge. No, *creeping* across the lounge, moving stealthily so as not to be overheard.

It wasn't Ella. The study was directly at the top of the stairs and even though I was fully focused on my work, I'd have heard her key in the lock.

Would I also have heard someone moving down the hall towards the lounge door? There was no other way in, and the new double-glazed sash windows were locked – I'd bolted them myself a week ago.

The creeping sound continued. Whoever it was had

left the relative insulation of the rug and was walking on the bare floorboards near the leather chair, padding slowly as though they wore socks but not shoes. Not even slippers.

The footsteps paused at the open doorway and I realised that, despite the chilly air – I hadn't put the heating on – sweat trickled down my spine, the ache in my back forgotten.

We'd sanded the hall and stairs but not got round to carpeting them. The footsteps began again, across the hall to the bottom of the stairs. Another pause. My desk faced the window, the door several feet to my right, the stairs out of my line of sight. It struck me that the maker of the footsteps wasn't creeping as such. It was more that they were struggling to walk, shuffling along slowly.

I waited, my heart a stone in my chest. The footsteps retreated the way they'd come, as far as I could tell. Then the lounge door banged shut with a crack as loud as a gunshot, making me bounce in my seat with shock.

Silence again. Next, from behind the door downstairs, I heard, 'No! NO!' followed by scuffling and a woman's muffled screams. Terrified of what I was an unwitting party to, I clamped my hands over my ears, tears gathering in the corners of my eyes. Yet I couldn't leave my chair, as though I were glued to it. The gulping screams continued but were getting fainter, ending in a drawn-out, husky gurgle that curdled the blood in my veins. Suddenly there came an almighty banging that felt like it was shaking the house.

I took my hands from my ears.

Thwack! Thwack! Thwack!

What on earth was that?

Again it came. *Thwack! Thwack! Thwack!*

'John? John! Where are you! I've forgotten my key!' My wife's indignant voice floated through the letterbox.

The brass door knocker! I wasn't used to the sound it made. Gratefully, I flew down the stairs to let Ella in.

'Love, you look like a wild man,' she said, peering at me. 'Your eyes are practically bulging out of your head. If this is the effect working late has on you, you need to tell Gavin you won't do it anymore.'

'I-I- er...' I couldn't think of anything to say. To my right, the lounge door was wide open, the mushroom cushion crumpled on the floor in front of it...

Ella confessed to one too many cocktails at dinner as I followed her into the kitchen. 'A few glugs of water in an effort to prevent a hangover tomorrow, then up the wooden hill to bed,' she said, taking a glass down from the shelf.

Lying together, we half-watched a mindless talk show on the bedroom TV and Ella soon drifted off, on her back with her lips slightly parted as usual, breathing steadily. I too lay on my back, taking comfort in my wife's warm body beside me and the chatter of voices on the TV. Back in the reality of marriage, feeling the solidity of the mattress beneath me and my head sunk deep into the pillow, I began to relax.

I'd been putting so many hours in at my desk that it was no wonder my mind was playing tricks on me. Ella was right. Gavin did work me too hard, taking advantage of my eager-to-please personality, now stronger than ever due to a fear of redundancy, which is how my last job had ended two years ago.

I felt my eyes close, and next thing I knew I was wide awake, the clock on the side table declaring the time to be 8:03. An early riser on weekdays and weekends, I climbed out of bed. Lie-ins gave me brain fog, whereas Ella relished them.

The stairs were cold under my bare feet, and I vowed to pin Ella down on a date to order carpet for it. Reaching the bottom, I became aware of a terrible stench: rotting food, no, rotting flesh, like the leftovers of a meat meal stowed at the bottom of the bin, gone but not altogether forgotten. Sniffing the air, I padded towards the kitchen, planning to whip out the offending black bag and stick it in the garden dustbin until bin collection day.

Inexplicably, the decaying flesh stink became fainter the closer I got to the kitchen. Reaching the bin, I pressed the foot pedal that opened the lid and bent over the yawning bin mouth. While the contents weren't exactly fragrant, the old takeaway wrappers and soggy napkins clearly weren't responsible for the stench. I let the lid fall and moved back along the hall, perplexed, the putrid smell picking up again as I walked. Was it the drains out front? A dead rat in the

THE DOCTOR AT CUTTING CORNER

cupboard under the stairs?

I stopped. In the hall, the side of the stairs was ahead, the cupboard under it to my right and the front door to the left. Tugging the cupboard doorknob, I poked my head inside, flicking on the light. At my feet was the vacuum cleaner next to a couple of unopened boxes from the move. My toolbox sat on the shelf at head height and the only thing in there to disturb my nose was dust, which made it twitch with an unexploded sneeze. Killing the light, I closed the door.

In the hall, the stench was as strong as ever. Turning this way and that like a bloodhound on a scent trail, my attention was drawn to the lounge. The door was ajar. I pushed it wider. There was the chair, the cushion back in place. Had I replaced it last night? Had Ella? Did it matter? It was just a bloody inanimate cushion, for God's sake. Yet as I took a step into the room, the stink intensified sharply.

Taking another step, I tripped on the corner of the rug, landing on my knees before the chair, forearms resting on the seat, my face pressed into the cushion. I couldn't breathe. The stench of rotting flesh was so overpowering I felt the bile in my stomach rise, rasping painfully in my throat and spilling into my mouth, the taste bitter and acrid, like mouldering olives.

In the few seconds before I scrambled to my feet, I experienced the sensation of the object being stuffed not with padding but with yielding hunks of rotting meat, as though someone had emptied a shovelful of flesh from an old grave in there. Racing to the kitchen, I vomited into our new butler sink, turning the taps on hard to swirl the bubbling strings of orange spittle and sick down the plughole. As I groped blindly for the towel by the sink to wipe my mouth, I felt a firm touch on my back and reared up in shock.

There was Ella. 'Vomiting in the morning? Are you pregnant?' Seeing my serious face, she patted my shoulder. 'Sorry, that was tasteless. Blame my hangover.' She gave a groan. 'Are you sick? You did look like shit last night.'

Ignoring the question, I said, 'Ella. Can you smell rotting meat or anything bad?'

My wife sniffed the air delicately. 'Nope. Although I can smell a sweaty husband who needs a shower.'

'Come into the lounge a minute,' I said, leading

the way. She followed, her slippers slapping on the floorboards. I pointed to the cushion on the brown chair. 'Smell that!' I ordered.

Ella looked at me, about to make another joke until she took in my serious expression. 'All right.' She picked up the cushion and sniffed it cautiously. 'Smells a bit of – old people's houses is the best way to describe it. Why?'

'No rotting meat?'

'Er... no...'

I snatched it off her. Yep – a slightly musty aroma that reminded me of my late gran's care home. Ella was observing me quizzically.

'I thought it had a funny smell,' I replied lamely. 'Never mind. Let's grab breakfast and go explore that park.'

The day was warm and fine for September and we had a delightful time strolling around the park. Near the end of our walk, we stopped at the lake to watch two swans gliding across the surface. But as we stood, it suddenly began to rain, slanting down hard, so the swans hurried to the shelter of the reeds and we ran under a spreading pine tree. A wind whipped up, lashing the rain against our thin jackets, the tree offering little protection.

'Let's get back and warm up with a hot shower,' I said, raising my voice above the wind. Hand in hand, we ran the few minutes home between the edge of the park and our house.

Upstairs, Ella showered first and as I waited my turn, I looked out of our bedroom window at the wet pavements, people hurrying past holding newspapers, shopping bags and anything else they had to hand over their heads as protection from the driving rain. A shower of droplets sparkled on the glass, covering the whole area and running down in rivulets that joined together until I could no longer see out. I shivered in my bath towel. Despite our cheery morning, I still felt on edge indoors.

Ella trotted out of the ensuite and made a playful grab for my towel. 'Mmm, Mr Wilkins! You'll be extra fragrant after your second shower of the day. See you in here...' She slipped under the sheets, beaming.

Afterwards, Ella brought up a feast of brie, cream

crackers and plum pickle, which we ate in front of a black-and-white Bette Davis movie. 'An ideal Sunday afternoon with my ideal husband in my ideal house,' she murmured, snuggling against me. I couldn't disagree. With the wind prowling the streets outside and the sound of the rain pattering against the window, I felt blessed and secure in a way I hadn't since before Dad died. The film hadn't finished but Ella had nodded off, on her back again.

Suddenly, I was alert. Was that footsteps in the lounge again? I snatched the remote from where it lay on the bed and clicked Bette off mid-way through a speech, my feelings of safety draining away like rainwater down a street grid.

Was the lounge door open or shut? I couldn't remember. But the soft, creeping steps continued across the wooden floor. Again, they paused at the door. Then they crossed slowly to the stairs, taking their time.

This time, the creeper began to climb, one painful step at a time in stockinged feet. I got the impression they were struggling, using the banister as an aid to haul themselves upstairs.

One third of the way up.

Halfway.

'Who's there?' I shouted – except I was so frightened the words caught in my throat and came out as a hoarse whisper, barely audible.

Whatever was on the staircase paused. There was a sound like a wheeze, an exhalation from old, tired lungs. Had it heard me? Was it put off from whatever it had planned?

What in heaven's name *had* it planned?

Behind me, wind lashed a torrent of raindrops against the windowpane, making me jump. Every nerve was strained, as taut as the rope of a hanged man.

The shuffling steps reached the landing. The upstairs rooms were arranged in a semicircle. First there was the junk room, then the study, then our bedroom. The main bathroom was on the far right. *It* was in front of the study, waiting. Two steps would bring it to our open doorway, which I could see from the bed.

It was early evening, amber light from the streetlamp outside illuminating the landing through the side window. Whatever dwelt there moved a little, catching the lamplight so it cast a shadow across the bedroom doorway.

A man-shaped shadow.

The shuffling came towards the door and entered the room stealthily – yet I saw nothing moving across the carpeted floor. Ella, still asleep, was on the far side of the bed near the door and, like when I'd been glued to my office chair the previous night, I could only lie there motionless as the soft steps approached us.

Then I either saw, or sensed, the shuffler. The elderly man whose features I'd seen formed by the cushion yesterday regarded me with a look of such malice, sparse white brows knitted together in fury, that I drew back mentally inside my own head. He smiled, sunken cheeks pushed high by a grin that taunted and terrorised me. Then he was in profile, leaning over my wife and grasping a plump, pale object before him with bony fingers.

Next, with a surprisingly quick movement, he pressed the cushion down on her upturned face. I could only watch Ella's hands fly up, flailing as she struggled to push the man off, to breathe. Like last night, I heard, 'No! NO!' followed by gasping and gurgling. Finally, a last rattling breath and she lay still, one arm flung above her head, the other outstretched and hanging over the edge of the bed, a grotesque parody of a ballet pose.

The man straightened up, shot me a triumphant look soaked in evil and dropped the cushion on the floor. Then he simply wasn't there anymore, in the same way darkness disperses the instant you flick a light switch.

I blinked to clear my head. Beside me, Ella snoozed on, her face rosy in sleep, arms by her sides under the duvet, oblivious to the tableaux she'd just acted out a role in.

Adrenaline raced around my body, making my heart bang painfully in my chest. I knew what I'd witnessed. I probably wouldn't sleep tonight, but I sure as hell wasn't going downstairs until daylight broke.

I fell into an uneasy sleep, or should I say I awoke briefly after what I assume was a bad (very bad) dream, then dropped off again. I wasn't going to alert Ella to the possible fragility of my sanity by relating my, er, dream. But she did remark, in the kitchen in the morning, that I seemed subdued.

It was Monday. In the front room, the cushion sat minding its own business in the chair, as cushions do. Ignoring it for now, I emailed Gavin to say I was working from home, fabricating a story about a blown boiler and waiting for a workman. I planned to confront the owner of the salvage shop and ask about the provenance of the cushions.

I saw Ella out of the door after breakfast, then forced myself to focus on the newspapers online while I waited for 9.30am to roll around – the shop's opening time, according to its website.

At 9.30am sharp, I appeared at the owner's shoulder as he fiddled with the releasing mechanism on the shop's metal shutters. After the horror I'd witnessed last night, I didn't plan to waste time on pleasantries. I went for the jugular. 'Excuse me,' I said, more aggressively than I'd intended. 'My wife and I bought a leather chair and four cushions from you recently. You said the cushions had all come from the same house. Can you tell me anything about the place?'

The man turned to look at me, surprised. 'Good

heavens,' he exclaimed. 'I can't remember every house clearance job off the top of my head. Let's get inside and I'll see what I can do.'

He took his time winding up the shutters, then fumbled in his pocket for the door key, during which time I felt my anger bubbling up. Inside, the shopkeeper placed his keys on the glass cabinet that served as a desk and brought out a ledger, which he opened flat on the top. As he leafed through the pages, taking his time, I longed to snatch it off him and do it myself. Biting back my impatience, I said, in as steady a voice as I could manage, 'Well?'

He looked up briefly at my rudeness, pausing as he traced a yellow-nailed finger across one page. 'Here it is. House clearance on the 24th of last month. One burgundy Chesterfield, circa 1934. A pair of mahogany wardrobes, circa 1900. One vase...'

'This is the house the cushions came from? What's the address?'

He glanced at me slyly. 'I can't share the address with you. It's confidential.' He raised an eyebrow. 'Why do you want to know, anyway?'

'Then why didn't you...' I began, exasperated.

Digging in the pocket at the back of my phone wallet, I drew out a £20 note and slapped it on the counter.

'I guess this is what you're waiting for. Tell me!'

Snatching up the money, he rattled off an address not far from my mum's house, which was across town. I only saw her twice a year as I found her digs and rude comments hard to deal with. I'd received one of her guilt-trip calls the other week asking when I was free. Happily, I could combine a visit to her with looking at the house the items came from and maybe grab a neighbour to see what I could find out.

'Before you ask, no, I don't know anything about the person who died,' he muttered. 'I'm in the business of making money, not listening to people's life stories.'

I was out of the door by now. 'I can tell you that leather chair your wife bought came from the same house, though,' he called after me.

Part of me wasn't surprised. Even more reason to find it...

In the name of helping the environment, Ella and I had long since ditched our car, so I texted Mum to say I was popping in and found a bus.

She still lived in my childhood home. Passing the old landmarks, I felt my spirits sink lower and lower the closer I got to the house. Mum had remarried, not to horrible Harry, thank goodness, but to some poor sap who hadn't realised how awful she was until it was too late and he had a ring on his finger. Nearing seventy, Alan still worked, to keep Mum in the style she was accustomed to as well as handily limiting the amount of time in her company.

The house had been much improved, thanks to her husband's generosity. Nevertheless, my mood dropped into my boots as I crossed the threshold and the memory of the 1,000 miserable days and nights spent under this roof before I'd managed to escape to my own flat flooded back. With a silver crop hairdo like actress Judi Dench and wearing her usual expression of barely contained scorn, Mum showed me into the back room as though I was a guest rather than her only child.

'What can I get you?' she asked brightly. 'Tea? Coffee?'

Accepting the offer of coffee, I bit my tongue as Mum chattered on about herself, not asking me a single question. Although I should be used to it after 33 years, it still irked me that she could be so self-centred and not realise it – or care. Did no one ever pull her up on this?

I let her words wash over me as I waited for her to take a breath, my opportunity to shoehorn in a bit of information about me and my life before she launched into Act Two.

'Ella and I love the new house,' I cut in when my chance came. 'We got a few items from a probate sale round the corner from here. Gilbey Road. I thought I'd wander over, see what I can find out about the occupants.'

Mum grimaced. 'Why you buy old rubbish when you can get brand new, I don't know. I'm off to the post office – it's down that way. I'll walk with you.'

Twenty minutes was about as long as I could stand with Mum and that was up, but I could hardly refuse her offer, given that I'd already said I was going to Gilbey Road. A wide, tree-lined street with houses much bigger than ours, we walked along it and I stopped in front of number 23. 'Is this where your second-hand treasures came from?' said Mum with a barely concealed smirk.

I nodded, peering over the privet on either side in search of handy neighbours who might be prepared to spill the beans on number 23's previous inhabitants.

Mum leaned forward and placed a hand on my chest, eyes wide in the way that meant she was about to impart juicy gossip.

'No!' she said, shaking her head in mock horror. 'This was old Harry's house – the man who used to live next door to us. You must have heard?'

Before I could reply, she continued, warming to the subject. 'I think you knew I was friendly with Harry after your dad died?'

'And pretty friendly with him before Dad died, too,' I wanted to say, but bit it back.

'He wanted to marry me and be your stepdad,' she simpered, 'but as I spent more time with him, I realised what a nasty man he was. Violent. Do you know, he whacked me in the face after I'd been to the pictures with my girlfriends? Said I was out looking for men. Ridiculous. Wanted to control my life and who I saw. Me, of all people!

'Luckily, I met Alan, so broke things off with Harry.

He threatened Alan on our doorstep and we were going to move away, but then Harry found a woman his own age – you know he was 15 years older than me – and settled down with her in this house. She was frail and suffered from severe asthma; maybe he thought she'd be easier to keep under his thumb. I didn't see them around, but I heard the marriage was far from happy. He couldn't stand her going out.

'The story goes that she told him she was leaving and he couldn't bear it. Now, this you must have seen in the papers? He smothered her with a pillow! Last year.

'He almost got away with it, because he said he found her having an asthma attack and she couldn't get her breath. Her son from her first marriage was asleep upstairs at the time – he found her, slumped over and blue in the face in an armchair. And you'll never guess which chair!' Mum leaned forward. 'That brown leather one of your dad's! Can you imagine?'

I was dumbstruck. 'Harry suffocated his wife – in my dad's chair? You've completely lost me. When I was a kid, you said Harry took it to the dump!'

Mum shook her head. 'I told you Harry was a

strange man. He wanted your dad's chair. "That belonged to the man of the house," he said at the time, puffing out his chest like a bulldog. "*I'm* the man of the house now Bert has gone, so I should have it." It seemed best not to tell you. He'll have taken it to his new home.'

I felt the blood drain from my face with shock. Not only did I have Dad's actual chair, but the full truth was too horrible to contemplate. I hadn't seen Harry for decades, so no wonder I hadn't recognised that sinister face immediately. My old neighbour had smothered his wife to death while she sat in my dad's chair! Using a cushion, not a pillow. And I knew which cushion.

'W-what happened to Harry? I asked falteringly.

'The death of Mildred – that was her name – was ruled to be due to natural causes, but her son pushed for an inquest. Harry died before the legalities could proceed.'

It was unimaginable. Mildred's son upstairs while the women-hating old goat crept around the house with murder on his mind...

'I see,' I finished. 'Got to run now, Mum.'

I got a cab straight home. To get shot of that chair and those cushions before my wife came to any real harm...

Newsletter & Free Exclusive Novella

One of the best things about being an author is building a relationship with my readers. Your support allows me to keep writing my books and I appreciate that. So do join my monthly newsletter and keep in touch. There'll be subscriber-only content, true hauntings and fascinating facts, plus you'll be the first to hear about my new books. As a sign-up gift, you get the exclusive novella *How I Wonder What You Are: A Ghost Story*.

What lurks in the shadows at Lukas's family home and what does it want?

When Lukas, Nicola and their small daughter Emily move to a quiet street, the family's peace is threatened when Nicola acquires a car, which resurrects Lukas's memories of his mother's death in an accident. Then Emily discovers a mysterious music box in her room and events take a sinister turn. As past and present collide, Lukas's life begins to unravel in ways he could never have imagined...

Visit my website **tinavantylerbooks.com** to sign up and tell me where to send your novella.

Bye for now!

To My Readers

I hope you enjoy this collection of spine-tinglers. If so, please consider leaving an honest review on Amazon to help fellow fear-fanciers who are considering buying this book. Thank you!

The Doctor At Cutting Corner And Other Ghost Stories is the fifth of my supernatural story collections. These are fiction, but my previous four books are of true ghost stories, the first being *Real Ghost Stories: True Tales Of The Supernatural From The UK*. Follow me on my Facebook page **@TinaVantylerBooks**, my TikTok **@SpookyTinaVT** or my Instagram **@tinavantylerauthor** for news and information about my stories and upcoming releases.

Also by Tina Vantyler

HAVE YOU READ THEM ALL?

Four books in the Real Ghost Stories series, available from Amazon:

True Tales Of The Supernatural From The UK

12 brand-new, modern accounts of genuine paranormal activity that you won't find anywhere else, including: A stroll in the park that turned to terror in *On The One Hand;* an anniversary break that almost broke a husband and wife in *Floored;* the dream home that housed a fiend in *The Bad Man;* the horror that waited below in *Going Underground;* and a reminder to be careful what you wish for in *Not In*

My Back Yard.

TRUE TALES OF THE SUPERNATURAL FROM THE UK VOLUME TWO

15 genuine heart-stopping encounters with phantoms and poltergeists, such as: The activity that terrified a paranormal investigator in *Bad Vibrations;* the former funeral parlour's foul visitor in *Up In Smoke;* the battle between feminine energy and masculine malevolence in *Someone To Watch Over Me;* the marrow-freezing expression of affection in *Different Strokes;* and the bloody pact that led to pandemonium in *Bonded By Blood.*

TRUE TALES OF THE SUPERNATURAL FROM THE UK & IRELAND VOLUME THREE

These 16 delightfully frightful, bone-chilling encounters with the undead will clasp you in a cold embrace and include: The mother so distraught she couldn't tell right from wrong in *Death Becomes Her;*

the terror wreaked by a jilted lover in *Full Throttle;* the merchant incensed by changes to his home in *Shop Of Horrors;* the nauseating stench that accompanied a ghastly guest in *Bedfellows;* and the disembodied head in the hall in *Visitors.*

REAL GHOST STORIES: TRUE TALES OF HAUNTED TOYS VOLUME FOUR

15 original true tales of toys gone bad and innocence corrupted, such as: The ghastly gift from a damaged playmate in *The Doll;* the demonic fiend that pursued a family in *Memento Mori;* the diabolical package from a dead mother in *Ol' Blue Eyes Is Back;* the small visitor from beyond the grave in *David;* and the sinister mystery man in the photo in *In Pieces.*

One collection of short ghost fiction:

THE DOCTOR AT CUTTING CORNER AND

OTHER GHOST STORIES: SPINE-TINGLING
TALES OF THE SUPERNATURAL

Six ghost horror stories to torture your mind with macabre images that will send icy shivers rippling down your spine, including: The surgeon with a bloody secret in *The Doctor At Cutting Corner;* the horror unleashed by accident in *Heads You Lose;* the vengeful fiend at a lonely train station on Christmas Eve in *Nipper;* and the gruesome act that lingered on in *The Ancestral Seat.*

ABOUT THE AUTHOR

The supernatural has fascinated journalist Tina Vantyler since she was a (weird!) child. The fact her mother kept her up late watching classic horror films and took Tina on outings to graveyards rather than playgrounds probably has something to do with her obsession. Several supernatural experiences of her own, along with the terrifying testimonies of people

Tina has spoken to, have confirmed for her that, as Mr Shakespeare said, 'There are more things in heaven and earth... than are dreamt of in your philosophy.'

Tina writes fiction and non-fiction about the paranormal.

Acknowledgements

Many thanks to Lis and Oliver once again for casting their eye over the finished stories. You are such stars!

Printed in Great Britain
by Amazon